D1350940

DR. MORELLE'S CASEBOOK

After a spate of time-wasting telephone calls, the Doctor had told Miss Frayle not to bother him with them; she must dismiss the callers and leave him to work on his thesis. But when the telephone rang again it was Professor Howard, clearly in the midst of a desperate struggle, wanting to speak to the Doctor on a matter of life and death. The Professor was being attacked — by spiders. So begins one of Doctor Morelle's strangest cases . . .

ERNEST DUDLEY

---- ◆ ----

DR. MORELLE'S CASEBOOK

Complete and Unabridged

LINFORD
Leicester

First published in Great Britain

First Linford Edition
published 2010

British Library CIP Data

Dudley, Ernest.
 Dr. Morelle's casebook. - -
 (Linford mystery library)
 1. Morelle, Doctor (Fictitious character)- -
 Fiction. 2. Private investigators- -Fiction.
 3. Detective and mystery stories.
 4. Large type books.
 I. Title II. Series
 823.9'14–dc22

 ISBN 978–1–44480–066–1

Published by
F. A. Thorpe (Publishing)
Anstey, Leicestershire

Set by Words & Graphics Ltd.
Anstey, Leicestershire
Printed and bound in Great Britain by
T. J. International Ltd., Padstow, Cornwall

This book is printed on acid-free paper

FOR
JANE GRAHAME

IN LOVE AND DEEPEST GRATITUDE
FOR HER PERFORMANCE AS THE
ORIGINAL MISS FRAYLE, AND IN
THE EVEN MORE ARDUOUS ROLE
OF THE ORIGINAL MRS. DUDLEY.

1

The case of the Escaped Wolf Spiders

Miss Frayle carefully dusted the ivory telephone, which stood on Doctor Morelle's impeccably neat desk. She handled the instrument almost with reverence, as she thought of the messages of drama and excitement it had brought to the house in Harley Street. In the mundane sense, the telephone was just a mechanical instrument. Doctor Morelle would explain in one sentence, she reflected, exactly with what simplicity it worked. But to her, it was a mysterious creature, alive and with a soul of its own. A human agency — and yet a sort of spiritual medium, which took on the mood and characteristics of the persons who used it. She thought of the many appeals for help that had come through on that instrument.

Shuddering slightly, as in her mind she

relived these bizarre memories, she wrapped the duster round a paper knife and inserted it under the metal part of the dialing contraption, in order to clean the numerals and exchange letters.

She almost dropped the instrument as the door opened abruptly, and Doctor Morelle, a sardonic smile on his thinly-etched lips, observed her with derisive disapproval.

'Do I detect you in the act of making a surreptitious telephone call?' he demanded, over-elaborately laconic.

'Indeed you do not.' A flicker of fire showed behind Miss Frayle's horn-rimmed spectacles. 'I was merely dusting it for you.'

'I would prefer that you would desist,' he snapped. 'Repeatedly I have informed you never to touch my scientific instruments.'

'But,' she protested, 'the telephone, it's — well, it's just a — telephone!'

'Irrefutably! Nevertheless it is also one of my most valuable scientific assets, Miss Frayle,' he retorted in acid tones. 'Without it I should be as helpless as — '

2

'As helpless as you would be without me?' she prompted brightly.

'That was not the simile I was seeking,' he responded. 'Please control your present pert mood, and kindly apply yourself to your duties with greater diligence.'

'Very well, Doctor.'

'In addition, Miss Frayle, it might be advisable to extricate your foot from the telephone cord. Otherwise, I fear dislocation of your spinal vertebrae is imminent.'

Gingerly she stepped over the wire, and while watching her feet, knocked the cigarette-stubbed ashtray from the desk. The contents scattered to the carpet.

'Pray repair to your desk before you completely demolish my sanctum,' the Doctor rasped as he stood over the confused figure of Miss Frayle who was now using a page from one of his research theses to scoop up the ashes.

Telling herself that it was indeed one of those days when everything goes wrong, she proceeded to her desk, making a rebellious moue with her lips as soon as her back was turned on the Docor. She sat at her typewriter, watching him obliquely through the mirror on an adjacent wall.

With an air of restrained martyrdom, Doctor Morelle reached for the telephone. Swiftly and precisely he dialled a number, and at the same time sagely commented:

'An ingenious though wearing device, this dialling system. I gravely portend that future generations will be born with abnormally developed indicative digits!'

He heard the click as he was being connected.

'Is that Mayfair 46892?' he asked tersely.

A bland voice at the other end replied: 'At the stroke of the gong, it will be ten thirty-two precisely.'

The Doctor regarded the mouthpiece with disfavour.

'Young woman, I shall report you for insolence,' he snapped impatiently. 'I did not ask you the time. Kindly inform me without delay if you are Mayfair 46892?'

'At the stroke of the gong — ' the golden voice began again sweetly, and

4

with an expression of bitter annoyance the Doctor realised that the voice was recorded. He crashed the receiver down on its cradle and a second later dialled again. Miss Frayle watched his irritation with concealed glee.

Again, the golden voice answered: 'At the stroke of the — '

Miss Frayle could scarcely hide her amusement now, but her delight at his discomfiture turned to apprehension as the Doctor, once again replacing the instrument, swung round in his chair towards her, and said coldly:

'Miss Frayle, this telephone seems to have changed itself into a verbal metronome. Can it be your tampering has damaged the instrument?'

'But, Doctor, I only — ' Before she could excuse herself, the telephone bell shrilled loudly.

'The breakdown department, no doubt,' he portended sardonically reaching for the telephone. 'Probably to inform us that your interference has dislocated all telephone lines between here and Edinburgh!'

He lifted the receiver: 'Hello — what do you want?'

A high-pitched feminine voice crackled over the wires with such discordance, that he moved the receiver away from his ear, and his finely-chiselled nostrils quivered in distaste.

The voice said:

'If you're the man wot brought me that stale white bread instead of the nice currant loaf I ordered, you're heading for trouble — !'

Exasperatedly Doctor Morelle jerked down the telephone. Then he rose from his chair, lit a Le Sphinx and regarded Miss Frayle with an expression of extreme displeasure for several moments. She cowed under the threatening storm.

'It seems,' he said at last, 'that for the remainder of the day I am to be the recipient of complaints resultant on tradesmen's negligence. I suppose it would be completely futile for me to ask you to suggest a remedy?'

'You might dial O,' she suggested, with a bright attempt at resourcefulness.

'With what purpose, pray?'

'They could test the line.'

'Doubtless,' he commented, 'and for the rest of the morning I should be compelled to listen to some voice pestering me with inane questions!'

'Well, later on I'll slip round to the post office and ask them to put it right.'

'Later on!' he echoed, his eyebrows arched incredulously. 'Do you imagine I can do without a telephone for even half an hour? Do you not realise that at this moment someone who is in need — whose life even may be threatened — might be trying to communicate with me?'

'Isn't that exaggerating, Doctor?' she put in with a sweet smile. 'After all, days — sometimes weeks — often pass before we get such calls . . . '

'Am I hearing aright, Miss Frayle?'

'I mean, usually it's just people you don't want to speak to who telephone,' she persisted, in the knowledge that that was a fact he could not honestly deny. 'You've said often enough you wished the 'diabolical contraption would desist from ringing'!'

7

This was too much for Doctor Morelle. He did not trust himself to make any reply. Instead he turned his back on her and snapped over his shoulder: 'You will repair to the telephonic exchange this instant — and you will run, that is if you could be trusted to do so without dislocating your ankle. You will instruct an engineer to have the mechanism in working order within the hour.'

Miss Frayle would be glad to get away for a short while from the study which reeked of efficiency and Egyptian cigarettes. She smouldered with self-pity and a sense of injustice. She paused at the study doorway, her right hand tightened round the door-handle.

'Doctor Morelle, I refuse to suffer in silence,' she announced stiffly, blinking through her spectacles with rebellious dignity. 'I think your accusation that my dusting the telephone was responsible for the breakdown was — ' She paused for breath.

'Was what, my dear Miss Frayle?'

'Was most uncalled for,' she finished and slammed the door before he could respond. That's one up to me, she thought as she raced down the stairs into Harley Street, expecting any minute to hear him calling her back for some sarcastic reprimand.

Half an hour later, she was casually making her way up the stairs again, and now she tried to control an insistent little smirk which quirked the corners of her lips.

The reason for her elation was evident when, a moment later, she unobtrusively entered the study.

'The telephone is now in working order, Doctor Morelle,' she announced brightly. 'The post office people say that the breakdown was caused by a technical fault at the exchange and apologise for any inconvenience to you . . . ' Then she added with brazen precision. 'My dusting the instrument could not possibly have damaged it, they said.'

His mouth curved into a derisive smile. 'Then you are completely exonerated, my dear Miss Frayle,' he murmured, 'and I portend that, unless I am to endure for the rest of the day your attitude of martyred superiority, I must apologise to you.'

'It couldn't matter less, Doctor,' said Miss Frayle airily.

'Nevertheless I do apologise — most abjectly.'

'Oh, thank you, Doctor.'

'At the same time I should state emphatically that although your tampering did not disorder the mechanism in this instance, that does not mean that such a contingency will not arise in the future.' His bland tone now had a bite in it. 'You will not handle the instrument except to answer it. Do you comprehend?'

'Yes, Doctor,' she sighed, and negligently patted her hair while she regarded herself in the mirror. 'I've got a feeling we're going to have a lot of time-wasting calls on that telephone today.'

'Your intuition — not being based on scientific rationalisation — interests me only to an infinitesimal degree. I feel a little less speculation and a more conscientious application to your duties would not be out of place.'

The telephone shrilled. Under the

Doctor's lynx-eyed and critical gaze, Miss Frayle was sure that she would drop the receiver. But she held it tightly and hoped for the best. She listened to the voice at the other end of the wire, and then turned to the Doctor.

'The *Sunday Clarion* would like your views on whether chorus girls make good wives, Doctor Morelle,' she announced sweetly.

That request from an over-optimistic journalist who was seeking material for a symposium was only the first of a succession of futile calls. A woman telephoned that she had lost a bracelet in Regent's Park, and could Doctor Morelle use his power of ratiocination to advise her how she could recover it? A rich prima donna offered £50 to the Doctor if he could cure her laryngitis within two days. A schoolboy on holiday telephoned to ask if Doctor Morelle needed an additional assistant. (He'd been given a detective disguise outfit for his birthday!)

Each time the telephone rang, Miss Frayle announced the request with an irritating manner of 'I-told-you-so.' This was more than Doctor Morelle could stand. He gathered together his papers and made for the door.

'I shall continue my thesis in the laboratory,' he frowned, 'which is conveniently sound-proofed. Do not put any calls through to my extension unless they are of the most vital urgency.'

Doctor Morelle's absence suited Miss Frayle admirably. She reached in a stationery drawer and produced a bag of acid-drops, and munched luxuriously. She eventually sank into the Doctor's armchair, with a detective novel, which intriguingly began with the cold-blooded murder of an employer by the sore-tried secretary. After lunch she returned to the book, arranging the armchair so she had only to stretch a languid arm to answer the telephone. They were all unimportant calls, and Miss Frayle thoroughly enjoyed herself in evolving ingenious ways of putting off the inquirers. 'This line is disconnected,' she would say, or alternatively, 'Doctor Morelle left by aeroplane this morning for Stamboul,' or 'Doctor Morelle is yachting in Regent's Park.' The warmth of the fire, and a temporary lull in the telephone shrilling induced in her a sense of drowsiness. The book fell to her lap, her chin dropped. Dusk threw a shadow over the quiet study, and Miss Frayle still slept on, each breath she took precipitating her spectacles nearer to the tip of her nose. The telephone shrilled, and Miss Frayle jerked from her slumber with such violence that her spectacles clattered into the hearth, fortunately not breaking.

Astigmatically she felt for the receiver. Still half asleep, she muttered her formula: 'I'm sorry, but Doctor Morelle left for the Antipodes this morning — '

'But he can't have done. That's impossible!'

Miss Frayle was jolted from her drowsiness by the agonised pitch of the man's voice over the telephone.

'What do you want?' she queried efficiently.

'I must speak to the Doctor urgently — ' the voice trailed away, and then returned with compelling intensity. 'It's a matter of life and death!'

'Who is that speaking?' There was no doubting the urgency of this call.

'This is Professor Howard. Get the Doctor if you can.' She heard a banging noise, and the man's voice shrieking: 'Get away — get away!'

'Hello! Hello! What is it?' cried Miss Frayle into the mouthpiece.

'I'm being attacked,' the man shouted. 'I cannot hold them off any longer. I am attacked — by — spiders!'

Miss Frayle dropped the telephone with a startled cry, as though a spider was going to pop out of the instrument at her. She raced out of the study, down the tapestry-hung corridor and pushed through the double felt-covered doors that led to the Doctor's laboratory. She saw his gaunt figure bent over some papers, but she wasn't put off by the expression of questioning irritation when he looked up at her.

'It's an emergency, Doctor Morelle!' she panted, holding onto her spectacles. 'Professor Howard — he's in some danger — on the telephone — '

'Professor Howard, the arachnologist?'

'The what — ?'

'Tut! Where is that switch?' He moved quickly and connected his extension with the main line. He spoke into the telephone:

'Professor Howard? This is Doctor Morelle.'

'Thank God!' came the fervent prayer from the other end of the telephone. 'Listen, Doctor, I want — your — your — '

'Yes, yes. I'm listening.'

'I want your help. Immediately!'

'What has occurred?'

'I'm speaking from my laboratory.' The man was making a great effort to talk quickly and coherently. 'I've suddenly been overcome with muscular cramp or paralysis, so that I am unable to move.'

'Yes — go on.'

'Fortunately I was near the telephone, and my speech is unaffected.'

'Can you summon assistance from inside your residence?'

'That is impossible.'

'You are alone?'

'Not exactly, I fear.' For a moment the

15

man's voice assumed a tone of desperate calmness. 'At the moment of the attack I was handling a receptacle holding several live specimens of the *Lycosa Tarantula*, which I dropped and smashed.'

'Yes.'

'The insects have escaped and I can see them. They are coming towards me. A score of them. Several are crawling on to my shoes, I have just the strength to shake them off. They're creeping back again . . . They'll attack me, Doctor Morelle. I can't hang on. Come quickly . . . quickly. It's . . . it's . . . ' The voice trailed away in a paroxysm of groaning and coughs. Doctor Morelle slammed down the receiver, and, catching Miss Frayle's arm, marched her towards the door.

She trembled under his grasp, her eyes blinking short-sightedly. 'Doctor, what's happened?'

'Quickly, we must hurry!'

'He said he was in danger from some spiders,' panted Miss Frayle, trying desperately to satisfy her curiosity and at the same time keep up with him. 'And that he thought — '

16

'Yes,' he nodded briskly. 'Apparently Professor Howard is alone and helpless in his laboratory with a number of Tarantula or Wolf Spiders.'

'Did — did you say Wolf Spiders?'

'I did. Miss Frayle.'

'Are they — alive?'

'They are.'

'Do they look like wolves? Are they — they . . . ?'

The Doctor refrained from commenting on such naiveties and Miss Frayle imagined the worst. She shuddered as she pushed through the door into Harley Street. 'How horrible! They'll kill him, won't they?'

'He may be dead at this moment,' he snapped as he glared mesmerically at the only taxi passing. He beckoned to the driver imperatively. The driver's gaze was averted, and just as Doctor Morelle was about to hail him, a woman appeared from a doorway nearby and called 'Taxi' insistently.

Not to be forestalled, the Doctor crossed quickly towards the taxicab as the woman was clambering inside.

17

'Why did that female have to hail the only cab just as I was about to do the same?' he muttered irritably as he hurried forward.

'She saw you beckoning, I am convinced of it. I saw her looking this way,' gasped Miss Frayle, steadying her spectacles, as she took two paces to his one.

'Does anything about that woman's sartorial style or facial expression strike you as familiar, Miss Frayle?' he queried over his shoulder.

'Why, it's — it's Mrs. Howard — the Professor's young wife. What a coincidence!'

The Doctor slackened his speed as he saw the driver about to start off.

'In scientific rationalisation we do not place much credence on coincidence,' he snapped.

'Still, it's awfully strange that Mrs. Howard should get the only taxi just as you are rushing to save her husband, and I think . . . '

Miss Frayle's conjecture was lost to posterity because the Doctor drowned her voice by calling down Harley Street:

18

'Mrs. Howard, do not proceed!'

The woman could not fail to hear him, and signalling to the taxi driver, she opened the door as Doctor Morelle reached the taxi.

'Pray accept my regrets regarding the imperative nature of my greeting,' he apologised, already getting into the taxi beside her and beckoning Miss Frayle to follow him. 'This appears to be the only vehicle for hire in the vicinity.'

'And you need it urgently?' Mrs. Howard raised the thin pencil line of her eyebrows inquiringly.

'Precisely. Strangely enough I wish to proceed to Carslake Terrace — where I believe your own residence is situated.'

'But actually I wasn't going home,' the woman said with a touch of petulance.

The taxi driver swung round from the steering wheel "S'all right, mum,' he called through the half-open window. 'I'll take you both to where you want to go in a jiffy. You said Victoria Station, and that's only just round the corner from Carslake Terrace.'

'Excellent!' the Doctor nodded, leaning

back. 'You will be able to alight at the station, Mrs. Howard, and Miss Frayle and myself will then repair to our respective destination.'

Miss Frayle sat insecurely opposite Doctor Morelle and Mrs. Howard and she pondered to herself why he had not told Mrs. Howard he was speeding to her husband's house, with the object of saving his life. She could not believe that his motive was to preserve Mrs. Howard from anxiety. That was not in keeping with his character. She decided to keep her mouth closed so that she might not let slip anything that would ruin his subterfuge whatever it was. She would keep quiet and just watch for clues, and do some deduction of her own.

She regarded Mrs. Howard closely. The Professor's wife would be a youngish thirty, and the professor himself must be quite sixty, she deduced. Mrs. Howard was expensively dressed, but with a little too much ostentation for good taste. Those voluminous silver fox furs which dangled from her slim shoulders; the crystal earrings and her ungloved hand which bore just too many showy rings — just a shade too much of everything. Her hair beneath her little fur cap was always too obviously coiffured, and the eyebrows were too thin. And her mouth — though it was lipsticked into a voluptuous cupid's bow — nevertheless held a hint of petulance. The typical pretty woman who's married a man much older than herself for his money, Miss Frayle summed up with what she hoped was judiciousness. 'She's spoilt, and utterly selfish.'

The taxi was now proceeding through Hyde Park in the direction of Stanhope Gate.

'Now that my respiratory powers have recovered,' the Doctor was saying blandly, 'I really must apologise again for inflicting the presence of Miss Frayle and myself on you in this manner.'

'But you're quite welcome, Doctor,' Mrs. Howard gave a charmingly synthetic smile, which clicked off the next instant. She gazed with preoccupation out of the window, and leaned forward slightly as

21

though she was willing the taxi to go even faster.

'Driver, can't you go more quickly?' she exclaimed irritably.

The Doctor turned to observe Mrs. Howard through half-closed lids.

'No doubt you are endeavouring to catch a locomotive?' he speculated.

'No — not exactly.' She paused in some confusion, and then quickly said: 'I was just meeting someone at the station.'

'And very creditably, you do not wish to be tardy for your appointment?'

Mrs. Howard gave a little laugh, which she cut off quickly.

'Doctor Morelle, are you actually cross-examining me?' she demanded. 'Or merely trying to make small talk?'

Miss Frayle saw the Doctor's lip tighten imperceptibly.

'I fear my social propensities are a little clumsy,' he murmured with repressed anger. 'Allow me to offer you a cigarette, efficacious in the soothing of nerves.'

'Thank you, I would like a cigarette.'

Miss Frayle noticed that Mrs. Howard's right hand shook as she lifted the cigarette to his lighter. She inhaled deeply, and then took several short puffs in the manner of a person who is harassed by some secret anxiety. She averted her gaze to the window again.

Miss Frayle then saw the Doctor shooting a warning glance to her as he held a finger up to his lips. Mystified, Miss Frayle nodded, but she had to clench her hands tightly to prevent herself crying out in warning at his strange action that followed.

With unmistakable deliberation, he transferred his Le Sphinx to his left hand then, when the taxi jolted, he dropped the lighted cigarette in Mrs. Howard's lap, amid her fox furs. A second later, there was an acrid smell of burning fur. Mrs. Howard looked down and, with a startled cry, she agitatedly half rose from her seat.

'Now look what you've done!' she cried angrily.

'A most regrettable accident,' the Doctor said quickly. 'Allow me.' He leaned across and brushed his right hand across Mrs. Howard's lap to knock the cigarette to the floor. His gesture also caught the handbag that rested on her knees, and as it dropped to the floor, the catch opened, with the contents spilling at their feet.

Mrs. Howard turned on him with ill-concealed annoyance.

'Really, this is too much!' she stormed, her green eyes flashing behind their veil of mascara.

'Most unfortunate. Most!' the Doctor muttered consolingly. He extinguished the cigarette with his foot, and bent down to replace the scattered oddments into Mrs. Howard's handbag, almost falling off the seat himself as the taxi drew up with a jolt outside Victoria Station.

'I think it's very lucky I've got here before some other catastrophe happened,' Mrs. Howard exclaimed, as she alighted from the cab. 'I only hope I don't have the pleasure of sharing a cab with you in future, Doctor Morelle!'

She snatched her bag from him furiously.

'Good evening, Mrs. Howard — and again a milliard apologies.'

'*Good* evening!'

The Doctor tapped sharply on the window. 'Driver proceed with all momentum to 22 Carslake Terrace.'

The taxi swung round full lock, and inadvertently the Doctor caught Miss Frayle's accusing glance.

'You tried to burn Mrs. Howard deliberately,' she said. 'I saw you and I think — '

'Silence, Miss Frayle.' He spoke rapidly. 'Would you kindly divert your powers of observation to another direction? Pray focus your gaze through this window and inform me if Mrs. Howard is still in visual range.'

She squirmed round to blink out of the narrow window at the back of the taxi.

'I can still see Mrs. Howard,' she observed, peering closely through her spectacles. 'She's standing outside the station. A man in a tweed coat is coming up to her. I can see his face — I think I know him, Doctor Morelle.'

The Doctor smiled almost encouragingly. 'Indeed. It appears you are being of some assistance for a solitary occasion.'

Miss Frayle's mouth formed an intrigued

O. 'He's talking to her. They're walking off together — arm-in-arm,'

'Singularly interesting.' He examined the tip of his Le Sphinx. 'And who is the man, my dear Miss Frayle?'

'It's Larry Trent!' She swung round in her seat as the taxi rapidly negotiated the corner.

'Am I expected to know the gentleman, Miss Frayle?'

'He's an actor, Doctor.'

'That elucidates why I do not know him — a theatrical person!'

'His pictures are in *all* the papers.'

'Apparently the journals are published with the sole purpose of printing his photograph!'

'Not quite that! But he really is very famous. The show he's been starring in has just been taken off after a record run.'

Doctor Morelle made an exasperated click with his tongue.

'Really, Miss Frayle, I am disinterested in theatrical tittle-tattle which reflects so deplorably the imbecilic tastes of the masses.' He peered out of the window at a terrace where the cream-pillared houses showed like gaunt sentinels in the light of the street lamps. 'Carslake Terrace indubitably,' he pronounced. 'Despite the encounter with Mrs. Howard, and the — er — singularly unfortunate occurrences resultant — we have made the journey with all expediency.' He glanced at his watch. 'Only ten minutes from Harley Street.'

'And the Professor's been there with those horrible spiders all this time,' she shuddered. 'I do hope we are not too late.'

He gave her an enigmatic glance.

'Then hurry, Miss Frayle, hurry.' With one movement he pushed her out of the cab, and handed the cab driver the fare. He moved quickly up the steps leading to the house, hammered at the brass knocker, turned the door knob and pushed, and then quickly wheeled round on Miss Frayle who had not reached the first step.

'Since Professor Howard stated he was alone in the house, we shall no doubt have to force an entrance,' he reached out a hand commandingly. 'Your shoe, Miss Frayle!'

'My — my shoe!'

'That's what I said.'

'But — but why, Doctor Morelle?'

'You will facilitate the Professor's rescue, if, instead of asking irrelevant questions you hand me the outer cover of your pedestrian extremity. Come, give it to me.'

A light of understanding dawned on Miss Frayle's features.

'I see,' she murmured brightly, 'you're going to smash the window with it.'

'I am amazed at your perspicacity!' he snapped, and grabbed the shoe from her hand while she hopped to the railing on one foot, and clung there for support.

Turning his face away from the window, which was a few feet from the front door, the Doctor held the shoe in his gloved hand and sharply cracked the heel just below the lower half of the pane. A crash of splintering glass echoed through the quiet street.

'Now to find the window-catch.'

'Don't cut your hand!'

28

'If anything could be calculated to cause me to do so it would be your hysterical warning!' he retorted as he pushed back the catch, and applied upward pressure to the window.

'Ah! That is it,' he murmured. 'The window opens easily.'

He shone his torch into the dark room. 'Now, Miss Frayle, you enter first.'

'Wouldn't it be easier — ?'

'Don't quibble, Miss Frayle — '

' — easier if I had my shoe?'

'Here, here.' He almost flung it at her.

'Thank you, Doctor Morelle,' she acknowledged sweetly.

'Go on, get into the room!'

'All right,' she murmured, and began the acrobatic feat of clambering through the window, with commendable speed. 'I'm getting in now. Mind your head when you climb through Doctor — Oh!'

The words had scarcely formed on her lips before she had cracked her head resoundingly on the window frame.

'In the same manner in which you are minding yours, Miss Frayle!' He gave a sardonic chuckle and clambered through the window with a dexterity so elaborate as to show up her clumsiness.

He shone his torch round the empty room, and then trained the beam on a closed door. 'That would lead into the hall,' he commented.

In an agitation of terror, she grasped his right arm.

'What is it?' He queried testily. 'Have you seen anything untoward?'

'Not — not yet,' she fluttered. 'But did — did the Pro-Professor say lots of those spi-spiders were running about?'

'He stated a number had escaped.'

She trembled from head to foot. 'Then — then they may be all over the house by now!'

'That is a contingency which cannot be ignored,' he conceded, freeing himself from her grasp and striding toward the door.

'Don't leave me, Doctor!' she cried in a frenzy. 'Some of those spi-spiders might even be in this room.' Her voice rose in tremulous pitch at the thought. 'Oh, Doctor — I must get out! Please, please! Let me get out!'

Doctor Morelle returned to her side. 'Pray calm yourself.'

'But they'll sting me! They're poisonous! I want to go home, let me — '

'My dear Miss Frayle,' he said soothingly, 'the species *Lycosa Tarantula* do not sting.'

She became slightly calmer. She breathed a relieved sigh. 'Don't they?'

'No, Miss Frayle, they *bite!*'

Uncontrollably her scream rang through the empty house. 'Oh, I can't bear it!' she sobbed, clutching at him for protection. 'The horrible, beastly, crawly things! Sometimes — sometimes I have nightmares in which they're crawling all over me!'

'Freud would diagnose that as symptomatic of a repressed libido,' he observed analytically. And then he patted her shoulder, almost encouragingly. He was not unsympathetic, he realised that hysteria has a scientifically psychological cause and is prone to attack the *femina humana*. 'Come, Miss Frayle. Come now,' he soothed quietly. 'I will carry you — then you will be in no danger from attack.'

Her sobs died to a quiet whisper. 'Oh

. . . oh, well, yes, all right then.' A new fear seized her and she inquired with almost childish mistrust: 'But you won't drop me, will you?'

'I will endeavour to refrain from so doing.' He bent and grasped her light form confidently. 'Allow me. That's it.'

Miss Frayle was already smiling bravely through her tears. 'Didn't realise you were so strong, Doctor. Are you sure you can walk with me?'

'My present pedestrian progress is not aided by a horizontal escalator, my dear Miss Frayle,' he said blandly, secretly flattered by her approbation of his strength.

She reached out a hand. 'I can open the door for you.' She was anxious to be of some assistance now that she felt moderate safe. 'And let me hold the torch for you.'

They passed into a narrow hall.

'There's a light switch here, Doctor. I can reach it. There! Now we can see where we are.'

Doctor Morelle blinked in the bright light. 'The door opposite would appear to lead into the laboratory.'

'Should — should I open it for you?'

'If you would.' They walked through the second door, and paused on the threshold, while Miss Frayle's hands hovered unsteadily over the switch.

'Depress the switch, Miss Frayle. As I conjectured.' The words escaped the Doctor with grim precision as he sent a scrutinising look across the room.

At the far end was a mahogany desk and upturned was a telephone, the receiver dangling on its wire towards the floor. A heavy dark-clad figure lay beneath the receiver, a stiffened hand half clutched upwards as though to grasp the instrument.

'We have arrived too late to save Professor Howard. You may perceive him, Miss Frayle, in recumbent position on the floor.'

Miss Frayle gazed with horror-stricken fascination for a second before she buried her head in the Doctor's shoulder.

'Is — is he dead?' she gasped.

'I fear so. *Rigor mortis* seems to have already tightened the muscular fibres.' He

33

lifted Miss Frayle higher in his arms. 'Please refrain from contorting while I place you upon this table. You may stand here, out of harm's way.'

'Oh, thank you, Doctor.'

'Now, Miss Frayle, I must vacate your immediate proximity for an instant while I examine the Professor.' He viewed the body from several angles. 'Hmm . . . the telephone receiver hangs from its cord near his outstretched left hand, so it would appear he succumbed immediately after he had telephoned me.'

'And we were too late,' cried Miss Frayle agitatedly. 'Poor, poor man. How terrible!'

The Doctor nodded in a preoccupied manner as he inspected the remainder of the room. His shoes crunched against some broken glass on the floor, and underneath a table he perceived an oblong box.

'Here is the broken receptacle which housed the *Lycosa Tarantula*.' He bent to pick up the box.

Miss Frayle gave a warning cry. 'Doctor! Do take care! One of the Wolf

Spiders may be hiding near you!'

Undeterred, he lifted the receptacle with his gloved left hand. 'There is, in fact, at least one of the genus Arachnid within the immediate vicinity,' he pronounced calmly.

Miss Frayle squeaked in fright and stood on tip-toe in the exact centre of the table — as far as was geometrically possible. 'Where? I can't see one! How do you know?'

'Because I happen to be peculiarly sensitive to the proximity of the species,' he responded calmly. 'I was at once made aware of their presence as I entered the room.'

'Well, please be careful, Doctor,' she cautioned anxiously.

'Your solicitude is indeed touching!'

'I was just wondering what would happen to me if you were attacked and killed by the beastly things!' she said. 'Oh, dear, I wish we could go!'

He half smiled placatingly. 'Now, just remain where you are, Miss Frayle, upon your table. If a *Lycosa Tarantula* should be attracted towards you, I will place myself in its path and endeavour to deflect it from its objective.'

She beamed at him. 'You're very brave, and thank you very much, Doctor,' she murmured gratefully, and then added with more feeling, 'but must we stay here any longer?'

'I regret that such must be the case.' He dusted his knees with the palms of his hands. 'It is essential before our departure I should telephone the police.'

'The police!' she echoed, with a puzzled frown. 'What for?'

Doctor Morelle walked across the room to the table, and looked up at her with manner slightly histrionic, which, on the whole, was excusable, since this was indeed one of his triumphant moments. He weighed up each word with a precision that was customary to him.

'We must telephone the police, my dear Miss Frayle,' he pronounced slowly, 'to advise them that a most cunningly-contrived homicide has been perpetrated.'

'Murder!' She clutched her throat and swayed slightly, but when she recollected she might fall, she pulled herself together, and instead of fainting pressed a clenched hand to her forehead.

'Homicide is the term I prefer. It has a less melodramatic intonation.'

'But — but all the same you mean poor Professor Howard's been murdered,' she persisted dazedly. 'And I thought — oh, dear! What with Wolf Spiders all over the place and now a murder! And me stuck up on the table like a silly statue or something! Oh, dear, I do think it's a bit too much.'

As though in a nightmare she heard Doctor Morelle dialling on the telephone in the hall, and his bland voice saying laconically: 'Hello? Scotland Yard? This is Doctor Morelle speaking. I wish to report I have found Professor Howard murdered in his laboratory at his home, the address of which is 22 Carslake Terrace, S.W.I. The perpetrators of the crime are — '

Miss Frayle pulled herself together, turned round from the table and called promptingly:

' — the perpetrators are Mrs. Howard, and Mr. Larry Trent.'

'Thank you, Miss Frayle,' said the

Doctor acidly, and to her delight he repeated her words into the telephone, though to her extreme puzzlement he added: 'You will be able to intercept them at Blatchwick aerodrome, some twenty miles south-east of the Battersea Bridge.'

★ ★ ★

Later, the Doctor sat in his comfortable chair in the quiet study of the house in Harley Street. He dipped his slender fingers into the skull which served as a cigarette container and drew out a Le Sphinx, pretending not to be conscious of the light of admiration turned on him through Miss Frayle's spectacles like two shining beacons.

'I was really of some assistance in this case, wasn't I, Doctor?' she queried, consciously feeling a justification to share his triumph.

'Despite the fact that you had to be literally carried to and from the scene of the crime you were not an undue hindrance,' he conceded magnanimously.

'After all,' she pursued, 'I did tell you

who the murderers were didn't I?'

'That was a foregone conclusion, thoroughly patent to the most moronic intelligence,' he said coldly. 'The motive also was only too obvious.'

'I know,' she put in brightly. 'The Professor had made a will in favour of his young wife. She wanted to run away with Larry Trent, but she knew that if she did that, then her husband would alter his will. So she and Trent decided to murder him.'

'Only too grimly logical,' the Doctor nodded. 'They poisoned the poor Professor, then contrived a diabolically ingenious — but to my powers of ratiocination — a thoroughly transparent alibi. It was in fact, one of the murderers — Trent, theatrical idol of thousands of imbeciles — who telephoned me, purporting to be Professor Howard whom he had already killed. I knew at once, of course, the voice was that of an impostor, although his impersonation was professionally capable. You see, my dear Miss Frayle, the impostor made the mistake of describing the spiders as

39

insects. Spiders are jointed animals, of the specialised order *Araneida* of the class *Arachnida*. No arachnologist would commit the elementary blunder of naming them incorrectly as insects.'

'Had you guessed he'd been murdered then, before we left for his house?'

'I had reached some such conclusion.'

'I wonder which of them was the more guilty?' queried Miss Frayle. 'I can't understand how a woman could murder anybody. It's horrible!'

'No doubt at the trial it will be established that Trent actually committed the crime,' the Doctor speculated. 'Whether Mrs. Howard was also an accessory before and after the crime will also be revealed, and whether she induced him to commit murder, or whether he sought assistance. That doesn't concern us at the moment.'

There were still a few more points that puzzled Miss Frayle. She asked:

'Was it only coincidence that Mrs. Howard was hailing a taxi-cab in Harley Street when we came through the door?'

'Indeed it was not. Mrs. Howard was evidently apprehensive after the crime.

Her manner — if you remember — was not normal. She evidently wished to see if we were answering the emergency call so that she could establish for her own satisfaction that the alibi was successful. In addition she may have wished us to perceive that she was some distance away from the scene of the crime.'

'What I cannot understand is how you knew Mrs. Howard and Mr. Trent were going to Blatchwick Aerodrome.'

'That indeed was a masterly combination of histrionic strategy and scientific deduction,' he retorted with a complacent smile. 'You will remember how the cab driver revealed Mrs. Howard's destination as Victoria Station?'

'Yes, I remember.'

'From that moment I suspected flight. I then had to know the destination of that flight. The only possible way of ascertaining that seemed obvious. I had to commit incendiarism upon Mrs. Howard's attire.'

'You dropped a lighted cigarette on her.'

'Precisely, my dear Miss Frayle. Then, while seeming to extinguish the minor conflagration, I purposely projected Mrs. Howard's handbag to the floor, at the same time slipping back the clasp. While I was replacing the articles in the bag, I committed — larceny! I purloined these!'

He held up two slips of blue paper.

'Continental Air Line tickets!' Miss Frayle announced admiringly. 'So that's where they were going.' She thought for a minute, then she asked: 'Tell me, Doctor Morelle, is it true a Wolf Spider's bite is terribly fatal?'

He smiled wisely. 'On the contrary, it would not kill you at all.'

'Then that's why you were so brave!'

He ignored her. 'I fear popular superstition has much maligned the species of *Lycosa Tarantula*,' he went on smoothly. 'It is relatively harmless. That is another thing which the murderer did not know.'

'You seem to support another myth, Doctor.'

'Indeed — and what, pray?'

Her eyes seemed to snap behind her spectacles. 'I think it's a myth and a downright fraud that you can tell there's a spider in the room, without even seeing it!'

A sardonic smile quirked his lips. 'Indeed. Do you really believe that?'

'I do.' She laughed whole-heartedly. 'Oh, Doctor, why do you always take every chance to pull my leg — ?' Her voice trailed off, as she noticed his expression change to alarmed apprehension. His eyes peered round the room as if seeking something. His nostrils quivered m a strange manner. 'Why, what's the matter?' she cried. 'You look most odd!'

His tone was evenly derisive. 'It is merely the peculiar sense I possess — which you dismiss, however, as mythical. This sense informs me of the presence of a spider in the study at this moment!'

In one agitated bound, Miss Frayle clambered on to her chair. 'Oh! Oh, where?' she shrilled. 'Oh, Doctor, please, you know I'm terrified of them! Where is it, please?'

Doctor Morelle chuckled sardonically. 'It appears that I have again successfully, metaphorically speaking, pulled your leg!' he said.

2

The case of the Eccentric Mrs. Beaumont

Nothing is more calculated to irritate a man who has the distinction of the prefix 'Doctor' than to be continually asked by all and sundry for free medical advice upon the varied and usually minor ailments that flesh is heir to. These hypochondriac inquirers seem to care little whether their victim is a Doctor of Science, Philosophy, or Theology. Every medical Practitioner who is introduced to strangers knows this irritation full well. Hardly dare he say: 'How do you do?' to the type of stranger in question without that person responding: 'Actually I have a most odd pain, Doctor. I wonder if I may ask your advice? Quite unofficially of course. I'm sure you'll be most interested . . . most.'

Such a gambit was certain to arouse

Doctor Morelle's volatile temperament by its most sarcastic expression. He loathes to be taken for an ordinary General Practitioner, for his many degrees and honours in the difficult and highly specialised field of neurology and psycho-pathology are a source of secret pride to him Such inquirers for gratis information upon everyday ailments get abrupt treatment from him. If he does deign to prescribe, it is invariably on the following lines: 'My dear madam, your condition is entirely due to strain on the larynx coupled with over indulgence in rich comestibles, and a mild, and quite uninteresting, degree of anxiety neuro-sis . . .'

'Really, Doctor,' the hypochondriac exclaims, thoroughly impressed, 'and what can I do about it?'

'Do not articulate for one lunar month. Repair immediately to your domestic residence, and exist solely on bread and *aqua pura*.'

Such advice is usually effective in choking off the inquirer, but on the whole, it doesn't lessen Doctor Morelle's chances of being asked for free medical advice by many strangers he has the misfortune to meet. In fact, this annoyance is one of the minor reasons why he shuns any social gathering. Of course and quite by the way, the major reason for his desire for isolation is that at an early age he discovered that the majority of his fellow creatures are of a very low order indeed. To the Doctor the world is divided into two classes — the crudely illiterate, and the pseudo-intellectual dilettante. Both types he summarily labels 'basically moronic'.

Of all the people he has been forced to meet, there is only one type who is able to stand up to him for any length of time. This is the one person in a thousand who, usually through thick-headedness and gross insensitiveness, will refuse to be abashed by his sarcasm and downright rudeness. This type of person was as potent an irritant to the censorious Doctor, as poison ivy to a boy scout.

One woman whom he had the ill-luck to meet was unique in that her personality combined both types referred to, types which the Doctor disliked most. She was a perpetual cadger for free medical advice, and also she was completely unsnubbable.

This woman was Mrs. Beaumont, the wife of a rich stockbroker. Ten years ago she had built a large house off Hampstead Heath, which Doctor Morelle was pleased to describe as 'a modern antiquity'. The stockbroker, not without wit and a certain flair for anachronism, had called the house Contango Priory. The monastic sound of the name was also not without its touch of bitter humour because although the Stock Exchange closes in the afternoon, the broker would not return to Contango Priory before eleven o'clock in the evening, and would then archly explain to his wife and her friends that he had been 'chained to the office desk all evening'.

Subconsciously, Mrs. Beaumont had her suspicions about her husband. When she was dreaming at night, she would sometimes hear a voice, not unlike her own, saying: 'I bet he's carrying on with that little typist in his office.' However, she refused to realise this consciously, and neither to her husband nor to herself did she indicate that she thought he was capable of marital infidelity.

Mrs. Beaumont was therefore a woman who had great conflict in her two minds. Insistently her subconscious was saying twenty-four hours a day: 'He's unfaithful,' and just as insistently her consciousness was saying: 'He's not.'

There was small wonder, therefore, that this conflict led to a neurotic condition of hypochondria, as a form of mental escapism. All this, Doctor Morelle realised full well, but he was still completely bored by Mrs. Beaumont. Her mental condition was quite common in such cases — and he was ever impatient and completely unsympathetic to both marital problems and orthodox diagnosis.

His one desire as regards Mrs. Beaumont, was to avoid her on all and every possible occasion. Had it not been for Miss Frayle's constant repetition of certain items of gossip concerning her, the woman would have passed from his mind. As it was he was to learn from time to time, via Miss Frayle, that Mrs. Beaumont was turning Contango Priory into a miniature show place. The summer house was to be converted into a *hacienda. Objets d'art* were being amassed in all the rooms. Elizabethan tapestries and old panelling had been bought; also a number of Dutch master-pieces. Mrs. Beaumont was developing a taste for boulle and ormolu and cut glass chandeliers. The gardens were to be re-planned once more. Bougainville plants were to be shipped from Mentone, and there was to be an Italian terrace. The impeccably kept lawns were to be re-laid at a slope to give the house more prominence. Mrs. Beaumont was, it seemed, displaying an escapist form of preoccupation in setting her house in order if only in the literal sense. On a grand scale she was becoming pathologi-cally house-proud.

One morning, after Doctor Morelle had dictated several thousand words of shorthand notes concerning a current experiment to Miss Frayle he repaired to his laboratory to conduct further experiments.

Judge therefore his annoyance, when he returned to the study after an hour's highly concentrated work to find Miss Frayle bent over her typewriter, her notes beside her and a virgin sheet of paper in the typewriter.

She jerked up her head with such startled violence that her spectacles almost fell from the tip of her nose. Surreptitiously, she tried to hide a tabloid newspaper which she had been reading voraciously.

'Oh, Doctor Morelle, I'm sorry I — er — ' she apologised in confusion.

'Silence!' he exclaimed angrily. '*Qui s'excuse, s'accuse.*'

'I beg your pardon?' she stammered.

'A subtlety, my dear Miss Frayle, which I ought to have anticipated as being quite beyond your limited powers of comprehension. You sedentate there admitting guilt of your neglect to duties, for I perceive you have not even commenced the transcription of your hieroglyphics . . . '

'No, I'm afraid I haven't started typing yet, Doctor.'

He smoothed the lapels of his jacket. Miss Frayle could detect that he was in one of his supremely pompous moods.

'Am I to assume that your interest in ephemeral outpourings by conscienceless sensationalists is more appealing to you than my scientific thesis?'

A startled frown crossed Miss Frayle's worried brow. So he had seen her reading the newspaper!

'I don't understand?' she evaded clumsily.

'I mean Miss Frayle, I detected your clumsy subterfuge in attempting to hide the daily periodical which you were reading.'

She avoided his mesmeric gaze, and it seemed that by not looking at him she gained a lukewarm courage because her mouth tightened slightly.

'I was reading the paper,' she admitted, 'and there was something printed in it that made me forget completely about my work. It was something that made me think.'

'You astonish me!'

'You see, Doctor, it's something I believe would make a case for you.'

'Very interesting!'

She disregarded his sarcasm.

'It's about Mr. Beaumont — you know the stockbroker who lives at Contango Priory. He was found dead over his office desk.'

'Indeed.' The faintest flicker of interest reflected in the narrowed eyes.

'Yes, Doctor Morelle, and if you ask me, I think it's odd.'

'I've no desire to interrogate you, Miss Frayle,' came the retort, 'but why should you think it is — er — odd? Mr. Beaumont died from natural causes, did he not?'

'It says here he did,' she nodded, 'but you can't believe what the papers say.'

'Hand me the periodical.'

The Doctor held the newspaper at a distance with a look of distaste as though he was handling some naked bacteria. He glanced nauseously at the heavy black print in the headlines. In one perusal, he assimilated the salient points of the report.

Then he gave that mirthless laugh which Miss Frayle had grown to fear. He flung the newspaper into the wastepaper basket.

'Does it not satisfy you that two medical practitioners, both of them thoroughly capable in their limited spheres, should testify, after conducting a post-mortem, that Mr. Beaumont died of a stroke resultant of high blood pressure?'

'I still think it's funny,' she insisted. 'He was such an active man: such a healthy, ruddy complexion.'

'Often a sign of high blood pressure.'

'Who would have thought he would be taken before Mrs. Beaumont?' she speculated. 'She was always moaning about her ill-health.'

'As for her, such people invariably outlive their spouses — indeed often live to be nonagenarians. It's a lamentable fact that those who have little to live for seem to live longest. Now, Miss Frayle, may I insist that you desist from your melodramatic fantasies and commence your duties — or must I stand over you to force you to do your work?'

'That's what the old slave drivers used to do,' she retorted, but she was careful that Doctor Morelle had left the study before she voiced this rebellious thought. Even then the enormity of her daring brought a blush to her cheeks.

Miss Frayle was deeply disappointed. Coupled with the shock of Mr. Beaumont's sudden death, she'd had feelings of hope that his demise might provide a case for Doctor Morelle, which might have given her the chance to get away from her typewriter and the endless dictation which had been her lot for the past few months. She had said the sudden death was odd — cast out her red herring, but the Doctor hadn't bitten the bait, and Miss Frayle had to resign herself to the opinion that Mr. Beaumont had indeed died a natural death — and, incidentally, resign herself to more dictation and shorthand transcription.

During the next year there were several cases that Doctor Morelle undertook with his usual success. Miss Frayle, however, still continued to nurse an intuition that there was yet to be the case of the Beaumont mystery in the annals of Doctor Morelle.

As it was to transpire, in this particular instance her intuition wasn't going to prove wrong, as it had almost always done in the past. The Beaumont situation was to develop as a first-class mystery.

After Mr. Beaumont's death, his widow went into deep mourning and complete seclusion. No longer did she entertain lavishly at her show place. Her staff of servants was dismissed, although the probate of her husband's will revealed that she was still a substantially wealthy woman (despite a highly significant legacy to his secretary 'for her sympathetic devotion to duties'). No more was Mrs. Beaumont seen in the vicinity of Hampstead Heath or further afield. She never ventured outside Contango Priory, somewhat to the relief of Doctor Morelle, who was no longer button-holed in Harley Street with her requests for free medical advice.

Miss Frayle often speculated as to what it must be like at the Priory now. How could Mrs. Beaumont keep the house in a livable condition without proper servants? What had happened to the art treasures? Had Mrs. Beaumont changed from a houseproud hostess in the grand manner, to a misanthropic hermit? What secret did the shabby walls of the old Priory now hold? Miss Frayle was insatiable with curiosity.

Imagine therefore, her feelings of suspense and excitement, when she answered the doorbell one morning to find a woman on the doorstep asking for the Doctor. She said she was Mrs. Beaumont.

Miss Frayle admitted her and with the eagerness of a schoolgirl, raced off to Doctor Morelle. Her eyes held an excited light when she burst into the study.

'Mrs. Beaumont is here,' she exclaimed. 'She wants to see you urgently.'

'Tell her to go away,' he snapped, without raising his eyes from his paper-strewn desk.

'But you must see her! She looks dreadful — ' panted Miss Frayle — 'And she used to look so smart — all those lovely clothes.'

'I do not perceive why I should give Mrs. Beaumont an audience simply because she has changed her sartorial mode.' He flipped his cigarette in a gesture of dismissal.

'She won't go away! She's sitting in the hall with the door wide open. She wouldn't come into the waiting-room because she said the walls would 'close in and crush her'.'

A smile flickered at the corner of his lips.

'Claustrophobia, indubitably.'

'What's that, Doctor?'

'Fear of closed spaces.'

'Oh, and she says she's not herself.'

'Not herself! Schizophrenia, doubtless; or, in your parlance, Miss Frayle, dual personality. An interesting combination of dementia.' He stubbed out his cigarette. 'I think I will see Mrs. Beaumont, after all.'

Even Doctor Morelle could not help feeling a certain pity for Mrs. Beaumont when she was shown into his study. Her old clothes hung limply round her shrunken body. Deliberately she avoided his searching gaze. Her thin, unkempt hands touched strands of matted hair absently. But behind her dishevelled appearance was a bizarre hint of her former elegance. Maybe it was the poise of her head, or the faint swagger with which she opened her shabby coat.

Miss Frayle had to strain to catch Mrs. Beaumont's whispered words.

'I had to come and see you, Doctor. I kept putting it off . . . You see I haven't left the grounds of my house since my husband passed away. But I've not been well. It's my heart. I get sudden pains.'

'Ah, yes,' Doctor Morelle nodded not unsympathetically. 'We must examine you, and detect the cause.'

After an examination with the stethoscope, Dr. Morelle resumed his seat and leaned back.

'Mrs. Beaumont,' he said, 'You are suffering from a cardiac condition known as angina pectoris.'

For the first time she met his gaze. Her eyes were like the lifeless windows of an empty house.

'Is it serious?'

'If neglected, it is. Now. Mrs. Beaumont, I can recommend a nursing establishment where you would be well looked after.'

The woman's sunken eyes rolled. 'I couldn't leave the Priory. Oh no that wouldn't do. I have so many people staying there I couldn't possibly leave them by themselves. They are my guests you see. I owe a duty to them.'

Before she could check herself Miss Frayle had blurted out:

'But, Mrs. Beaumont, you have no guests there!'

Doctor Morelle spun round on her, so that her spectacles almost fell off as she jumped in fright.

'Silence, Miss Frayle!' He turned a dissembling smile to Mrs. Beaumont. 'Pray ignore the interruption. You were saying about your guests?'

'My guests! Oh yes . . . ' She seemed to be gathering together her rambling thoughts. 'Some of them have been with me for two years. There's such a lot of them. A real houseful. They talk to me by the hour. They keep me cheerful.'

Doctor Morelle leaned forward. 'Tell me, precisely who — or what — are these guests of yours?'

'I can't tell you.' Mrs. Beaumont's voice rose. 'I didn't come here to be questioned. It's no business of yours. I only consulted you because of my heart. Can't — can't you give me something for the pains?'

'Certainly.' The Doctor walked to a pharmaceutical cabinet, and took a small box from a shelf.

'This is amyl nitrate in capsule form. Whenever the pains commence, you must break the capsule in a handkerchief and inhale. Is that quite clear?'

She almost snatched the box from his hand. 'I shall have to run home now. You see my guests are waiting — '

She stopped abruptly as she saw another question forming on Doctor Morelle's lips. Then, with a neurotic burst of energy, she ran from the room and out of the house.

'Well I never!' Miss Frayle gasped. 'However could a woman change so much? In the old days she was always pestering you, talking about herself, and her ailments, and now — '

'Merely a switch of personality. Mrs. Beaumont has become another person.'

'Don't you think she ought to be looked after by someone?'

'The thought had not escaped me. However . . . ' He dismissed the subject abruptly, and turned to her. 'Now, Miss Frayle, I wish to dictate to you for the rest of the morning.'

She groaned inwardly.

She was still transcribing her shorthand notes at midnight. Her back ached with sitting in one position, and at the end of a page she would rise from her chair, stretch her arms, and with a tired sigh return to her work. She was about to insert another sheet of quarto in her machine, when the telephone bell rang with that sinister insistence which to her it always assumed after midnight.

She lifted the receiver exhaustedly. But as she listened her weariness vanished.

'Yes, yes!' she repeated excitedly, 'I'll tell him . . . right away. What's that . . . ? Oh, the poor soul . . . Yes, terrible!'

She burst into the Doctor's laboratory without knocking, and saw him scrutinising a pale green liquid in a test tube against the light.

'Oh — er — excuse me, Doctor — but — '

He didn't even look at her. 'Cannot you see I am working?' he snapped.

'I'm sorry — but well — ' she paused breathlessly.

'Don't stand there mumbling! What is it?'

'I think something must have happened to Mrs. Beaumont,' she gasped.

'A midnight intuition of yours, Miss Frayle?'

'No. Her gardener just telephoned. He wants to know if you'd go along there immediately. He seemed worried and . . . '

'Do not waste time with suppositions.' He was already stripping off his white laboratory jacket. 'Have my coat and hat ready and my bag — and stick. Hurry, Miss Frayle — hurry!'

Five minutes later Doctor Morelle was steering his car through the dark night. A heavy downpour turned the windscreen into a miniature stream, and the mechanical wipers threshed with greater urgency as he accelerated. Miss Frayle sat on the edge of her seat, her hands clasped apprehensively.

'How, I am constrained to wonder, did the gardener discover there was something wrong with Mrs. Beaumont,' the Doctor speculated. 'She allowed no one near her at any time. Odd. Distinctly odd.'

'The gardener didn't explain over the 'phone,' volunteered Miss Frayle. 'Look out, Doctor ... Slow up ... The turning's here.'

'Of that I was quite aware,' he snapped, with only a slight degree of truth, braking the car with such suddenness that it conveniently skidded in a half-circle into a driveway — more by accident than design.

The car ploughed and jogged through mud and cartholes.

'Dreadful road for a car,' he commented. 'Fortunately the house is relatively near.'

The headlights picked out the wrought-iron gates, which for the first time in two years were open. The car was now moving rapidly up the short entrance-drive, which was overgrown and neglected. Now the headlights shone on the Priory walls, covered with lichen and ivy. The front door was ajar, fixed by a chain that rattled in the wind.

Switching on a torch, the Doctor led the way into the house. Both of them stood on the threshold transfixed by the strange sight.

'The place is absolutely falling in!' exclaimed Miss Frayle.

'It is in a somewhat advanced state of decay.'

Miss Frayle pointed to an outer wall. 'Look, all this ivy, growing *inside* the house, through the window. There aren't any panes in the window frames — and look! All those little shapes in the shadows. They seem to be moving.' She tried to stifle a shriek. 'They *are* moving. Oh, Doctor!'

'Control yourself, Miss Frayle.'

If she had dared, she would have clung to him for protection. A second later she did reach out to him, as an eerie hooting sound came from just above her head.

'Oh, what was that?'

'Merely a nocturnal bird of prey of the order *Striges*,' he calmly explained, 'of which there are some two hundred species.'

The creature hooted eerily again.

'It's an owl!' announced Miss Frayle, with a gasp of relief.

'Precisely!'

'And there seem to be other birds here in the house.'

They could hear a chorus of awakened bird-life within.

'Apparently,' nodded the Doctor. 'Mrs. Beaumont extends in every sense of the term an open house to various feathered species. Let us investigate and her ornithological keenness will be evident.'

'Do you think she meant these birds when she said her house was full of guests? She said they talked to her and — '

'The conjecture had already crossed my mind,' he said, moving forward a few paces.

'How creepy!' shuddered Miss Frayle.

'It's so dark — and oh, there are birds everywhere!'

Doctor Morelle flashed his torch round the tapestry-covered walls. Priceless Dutch paintings were covered with cobwebs. Dust lay thick on the period furniture, and everywhere there were birds moving and chattering, and flying overhead, their wings making a continued fluttering and whirring, 'Observe the incongruous choice of perches,' the Doctor noted. 'Those crows on the chandelier, the sparrows round the picture rail.' He gave a chuckle. 'And this owl about to roost on your head, my *dear* Miss Frayle!'

This time she did not check her scream.

'Do something! Drive it away, Doctor.'

He clapped his hands, and the dusty whirr of wings passed to the other side of the room.

'Quite harmless,' he explained. 'No doubt Mrs. Beaumont has tamed these creatures. The owl wished to be friendly.'

'Thank Goodness, it's gone!'

He was shining his torch up the stairs that led to the minstrel gallery, and moved forward.

'Wait for me, Doctor! Don't leave me here!'

'Hurry, then . . . '

At the top of the stairs Doctor Morelle switched off the torch. 'Ah, a light, I perceive,' he murmured. 'It's shining under that door. The bathroom, doubtless.'

He banged his stick three times against the door. 'Mrs. Beaumont,' he called. There was no reply. He turned the door handle. 'Hm . . . the door is open. Wait there, Miss Frayle.'

'Very well, Doctor.'

'And do not be alarmed by that swishing noise you hear. It is merely the motion of a species of Chiroptera.'

'You're wrong, Doctor — it's a bat,' Miss Frayle declared in meek triumph.

'Consult the Encyclopaedia Ornithologia and you will find I am right.' Chuckling sardonically, he entered the bathroom, closing the door behind him. The eeriness of the house was too much for Miss Frayle's overstrained nerves. She kept on imagining that little creatures were about to alight on her hair, and tangle it with tiny claws. Then she would have to have them cut out of her hair, and it would be weeks before the hair would grow again. She had heard of such things happening.

She could keep quiet no longer. 'C-could I come in?' she called through the door. 'Bats are flying round my head!'

The Doctor opened the door slightly.

'Even so, Miss Frayle, I think you would prefer to stay outside,' he retorted enigmatically. 'Mrs. Beaumont makes an uninviting picture.'

'Mrs. Beaumont! What's happened to her?'

'She is in the bath,' came the reply, in a tone that to Miss Frayle always presaged news of disaster. 'She is face downwards in approximately six inches of water.'

'Do you mean she's dead?'

Doctor Morelle ignored Miss Frayle's unnecessary question. 'The water is ice cold,' he observed. 'Extraordinary.'

'But this is terrible.' Miss Frayle wrung her hands tensely. 'Mrs. Beaumont dead!'

'It is indeed regrettable,' agreed the Doctor. 'For the first time in her life, Mrs.

Beaumont was becoming an interesting patient.'

'How can you be so — callous!' she burst out. 'Anyone would think — '

'Silence!' He raised a warning hand and stood silent.

Miss Frayle listened and she heard the clanging of an iron-studded door, followed by footsteps over creaking floorboards and, growing louder and louder, the sound of someone whistling an old sea shanty.

Doctor Morelle put his mouth close to Miss Frayle's ear. 'Do not make a sound,' he whispered. 'Stand behind this pillar.'

But the precaution was unjustified, because the next second a bellowing, hearty voice echoed round the minstrel gallery:

'Anybody there? Doctor Morelle! Ahoy there!'

'I think it's Selby, Doctor,' Miss Frayle announced in a low voice. 'He's the gardener — the man who telephoned.'

Doctor Morelle moved from behind the pillar and shone his torch down the stairs. 'Stay where you are, I'm coming,' he called. Miss Frayle followed him apprehensively.

At the bottom of the stairs stood a man of heavy build bearing a storm lantern. A smile crossed his weather-beaten features as he greeted them.

'I saw the car and heard voices,' the man said. 'Are you Doctor Morelle?'

'I am, and this is my assistant, Miss Frayle.'

'Good evening, Doctor and Miss.' The man respectfully removed his cap. 'You'd be the young lady wot I 'phoned?'

Miss Frayle nodded

'And you are Mrs. Beaumont's gardener, I presume?'

'S'right. Selby's the name. Odd job man and all. Used to be at sea afore I came to work with Mrs. Beaumont. 'Ave you seen the old lady? Is she bad?'

'I regret to say Mrs. Beaumont is dead.'

'She is?' Selby echoed.

The Doctor trained the torch fully on the gardener's face. 'You appear not to be surprised?'

The other blinked. 'No, can't say as I am.'

'And why?' the question was like a whip-crack.

'Felt it in me bones somethink was amiss when I saw the light from the bathroom. It was on when I went to bed. I sleeps in an 'ut at the end of the garden, but I 'appens to wake up couple of hours later and the light's still burning.'

'Proceed.'

'Well, knowing how it wasn't like Mrs. B., I 'ops out of my bunk, dresses quick and goes round to the 'ouse. I calls, but there's no answer.'

'You didn't enter the house?'

'Ho no!' Selby's tone was almost shocked. 'That'd be more'n me job was worth. She wouldn't 'ave no one in 'ere but 'er blinking birds. I walks round the 'ouse, and the light's still burning. So I gets on the blower to you.'

Doctor Morelle eyed him with distaste. 'I presume you mean telephonic communication?' he said. The other nodded.

'That would be at a quarter past midnight, would it not?'

''S right, about that.'

'Yes, that *was* about the time,' Miss

71

Frayle corroborated but the Doctor ignored her and continued quickly in his interrogation.

'And from where, Selby, did you telephone?'

'Not from this 'ouse, 'cos two years ago, when the old skipper croaked — beggin' your pardon, Doctor and Miss — I mean passed away — Mrs. B. cut all the telephone wires wiv a pair of garden shears she borrered from me.'

Doctor Morelle's voice was that of a fractious schoolmaster when dealing with a singularly moronic child. 'I am still asking you from where you telephoned?'

'From a neighbour's,' Selby replied, crushed.

'I was not aware Mrs. Beaumont had any neighbours.'

'Only one. There's a cottage down in the hollow across the drive. It's rented by a Mr. Dexter. The fence has broken down. I can't keep everywhere in repair you know. So I 'ops through and it's only a few yards to Mr. Dexter's cottage, and I knocks at his door and 'phones from there.'

The Doctor thought for a moment, staring contemplatively at the ceiling through a cloud of cigarette-smoke.

'Did you have to disturb Mr. Dexter's nocturnal slumbers?' he asked.

'I didn't 'ave to get him out of his bunk, if that's what you mean. He was sitting in his front room, doing some writing, 'is 'air all over the place.'

The Doctor nodded briskly. 'Let us hope Mr. Dexter will not have retired to bed by now. I'm afraid we shall need to trespass upon his hospitality again — to telephone the police.'

Selby jumped visibly. 'The perlice? You don't meanter say — why, it ain't — '

'There are bruises on the back of Mrs. Beaumont's neck,' the Doctor announced calmly, 'bruises indicative of violence.'

Miss Frayle gasped in horror. 'You mean it was — ?'

'Precisely. Despite the fact that Mrs. Beaumont was suffering from a cardiac condition which might cause a fatal collapse, and also that the capsules I prescribed for her are still unused on the bathroom shelf, I am driven to the conclusion that she was *murdered*.' He turned to the other. 'What do you think of that, Selby?'

'I dunno what to fink I'm sure. No one would wish the old girl 'arm. She was cracked, but she were good-hearted.'

'Whom do you think — m-murdered her?' stammered Miss Frayle.

'That I shall inevitably elucidate, doubtless in a very short while,' replied the Doctor with an over-elaborate yawn of boredom. 'Meanwhile if you will remove yourself from Selby's path, my dear Miss Frayle, perhaps he will show us the way to Mr. Dexter's cottage.'

With the gardener leading, they walked round the house, and through some undergrowth, Miss Frayle constantly tripping, and being a general hindrance. Her hair was tousled by the wind and rain, her stockings laddered and her spectacles so blurred she could see no more than a yard ahead.

'Let me help you, Missy,' Selby volunteered kindly. 'Just take 'old of my arm.'

Gratefully, she held on to him. There

was something steadfast and human about the old man that completely won her confidence.

Doctor Morelle, striding sure-footedly through the blackness, turned abruptly to Selby.

'Has this man Dexter inhabited the cottage long?' he asked.

'For the last six months, Doctor,' Selby declared. ''E's one of them h'author blokes you know. Writes thriller stories for them 'orror magazines. Cheery sort, though, to meet.'

Doctor Morelle adroitly ducked under a low-hanging bough.

'Interesting,' he commented. 'Latently sadistic type, I presume.'

'What's that?' gaped Selby.

'The Doctor means,' explained Miss Frayle with the faintest touch of condescension, 'that Mr. Dexter probably has a dormantly cruel nature which he expresses in his stories.'

The Doctor chuckled. 'Thank you, Miss Frayle.' Again his thinly veiled sarcasm was in evidence.

Within a few minutes they were at the

cottage door, which was opened immediately at the Doctor's first knock. A cheery fire blazed in the open grate. Papers were strewn over a deal table in the middle of the room.

''Fraid I've a bad habit of working at night,' Dexter greeted. 'Do gather round the fire — please, and warm yourselves.'

Almost telegraphically Miss Frayle found herself summing up the author. Hearty type. Beer drinker. Good teeth, which would invariably clench a pipe. Middle-aged. Wore tweeds that had a heathery smell. Almost too disarming to be beyond suspicion, she thought knowledgeably, and she moved from his side to the comforting proximity of the old sailor, Selby, now turned gardener.

Doctor Morelle was explaining the reason for their presence while Dexter pulled at his pipe. When the Doctor had described what had happened at Contango Priory Dexter ran a large hand through his tangle of dank hair.

'This is a grim business, Doctor,' he observed. 'Why, it was only this evening I saw the old girl in the garden feeding her birds.'

The Doctor lit the inevitable Le Sphinx, and with half-closed eyes observed the author through the curling, blue smoke.

'You were not personally acquainted with Mrs. Beaumont?'

'No.' Dexter lit a spill for his pipe. 'Selby here will tell you she never spoke to anyone if she could help it.'

Selby nodded. 'S'right, sir.'

Miss Frayle shuddered. 'What a queer woman she was, poor thing.'

Dexter was drawing his pipe. 'Yes, I always said I'd put her in a story one of these times. Make a basis for a really colourful character, I reckoned. You know, eccentric recluse, interested in nothing but birds, found murdered in — well — ' he paused, 'well in similar circumstances to poor Mrs. Beaumont.'

The Doctor pounced on him.

'I have not so far described the circumstances in which I found the deceased,' he snapped.

The other hedged. Miss Frayle watched him with what she intended to be lynx-eyed scrutiny. Guilt written all over his plausible face, she thought!

'Well, what I mean,' Dexter explained, 'is that it'd be something like that in my story.'

'Nor have I stated positively in your presence that hers is a case of homicide.'

Dexter laughed. 'It'd have to be for me — all my yarns are about murder.'

'I see.'

Selby turned his homely face from the fire. 'Now I come to think of it, Mr. Dexter, I read one of your stories where the person wot was done in was also found in half a foot of water in 'er bath.'

'You must be mistaken,' denied Dexter quickly, 'I certainly don't remember writing any story with that happening. Though I must say a really juicy murder with plenty of blood and — '

Miss Frayle shuddered. Didn't the brute have any feeling?

'Isn't it rather gruesome talking like this,' she broke in, 'with that poor woman lying there dead.'

'Ah, it is,' Selby muttered with reverence. 'Rest 'er pore soul.'

Dexter turned swiftly to Miss Frayle. 'I'm sorry. I'm afraid I allowed my professional instincts to get the better of me,' he apologised.

Doctor Morelle eyed the tips of his shoes idly. He stifled a yawn only with an effort.

'Perhaps then, with your permission, you would allow Miss Frayle to telephone the police?'

Dexter waved his pipe towards the instrument that was hedged round with current crime novels. 'By all means, go ahead.'

'Just a moment, Miss Frayle.'

'What is it, Doctor?'

'Kindly pass me my walking-stick.'

'Y-your walking-stick?'

'Come along, please! Don't stand there like some astigmatic parrot!'

Dexter rose to his feet. 'What's the matter, Doctor? Leaving us?'

'Only when the police arrive, Mr. Dexter. In the interim — ' Doctor Morelle paused as he firmly took the walking stick from Miss Frayle, 'pray observe that by simply unscrewing the handle so — ' He pulled vigorously and revealed the narrow gleaming sword-blade.

'A sword-stick!' Dexter backed away apprehensively, as the Doctor flourished the blade through the air.

'Now, Miss Frayle,' he ordered, 'kindly lock the door. Come on, come on!'

'Yes, Doctor!' Miss Frayle almost tripped over herself to obey him.

'I'll have the key — thank you. Perhaps you two gentlemen will sit down quietly. Proceed with your telephoning, Miss Frayle.'

Agitatedly she gripped the instrument, keeping one eye on Mr. Dexter to make sure that he was well covered by the sword-stick, before she started tremblingly to dial.

'Is — is that Exchange?' she faltered. 'Could I — ? Would you put me on to the police, please? At once — it's urgent — the police. I'm speaking for Doctor Morelle. He has a murderer under lock and key here. The murderer is a Mr. Dexter. He's an author and — '

Doctor Morelle moved with surprising

swiftness across to the telephone and snatched it from Miss Frayle's hands. With his free hand he still gripped the sword-stick menacingly facing the two men.

'Dolt! Ignoramus!' he snapped at Miss Frayle. Then he spoke into the telephone: 'Doctor Morelle speaking. My irresponsible assistant has just made — completely without my sanction — a slanderous accusation. True, I am holding a murderer here, but the name is not Dexter. It happens to be Selby — the gardener at Contango Priory . . .'

★ ★ ★

Next morning, Miss Frayle was still a bundle of nerves.

'To think, Doctor,' she fluttered, 'that I was holding Selby's arm all that time. And he was a murderer!' She shuddered: 'I can't see how you can have known.'

'Simplicity itself.' Doctor Morelle permitted himself a superior smile. 'Merely a matter of deduction.' He smiled thinly. 'In fact,' he murmured, 'if I had been mentally lazy, as I never am, I could have deduced the murderer by just watching you, Miss Frayle.'

'Watching me?'

'Exactly. There were two subjects — the gardener and Dexter the author. Your attitude clearly showed that you, with your tedious intuition, suspected Dexter as the murderer. On the almost scientific assumption that your intuition is infallibly wrong, I could quite safely have branded Selby as the culprit.'

'Then I did help you, after all, Doctor?' Miss Frayle smiled at him brightly.

'I preferred not to be mentally somnolent! Therefore I used scientific rationalisation to solve the mystery. Quite plainly at least to me, the murderer of Mrs. Beaumont was the gardener. As it transpired, he gained nothing by his brutal crime for the wealth which he had concluded his employer hoarded was in fact safely deposited in her bank.'

'But how did you know he did it?'

'The vital clue that revealed him as the perpetrator of the crime was contained in his remark to Dexter. He declared he had read a murder story of the author's wherein the victim was also found in half a foot of water. The one word 'also' showed Selby was aware Mrs. Beaumont had been discovered in like circumstances, a fact he could not have known unless he knew more about her death than he had professed at the time. Owing to her fear of fainting the woman habitually used only a small quantity of water in her bath,' he added at a tangent.

Miss Frayle suddenly jumped to her feet. Her expression of open-mouthed attention changed to horror. Doctor Morelle regarded her with profound irritation.

'Now, what is it, Miss Frayle?'

'A bat! Something fluttering round my head! Oh, please drive it away!'

'Do not be ridiculous,' snapped the Doctor. 'It is merely a species of the *Lepidoptera* order, of which there are — '

'Oh, it's only a moth!' she sighed with relief. 'It did frighten me!'

He rounded on her with his customary scathing tongue.

'Why must you insist, my dear Miss

Frayle, upon reducing my scientific terminology to words of one syllable?'

'I'm sorry.' A worried frown crossed her brow. 'I wonder if Mr. Dexter will sue me for slander or something awful because I called him a murderer?'

'Fortunately for you,' he smiled, 'I think not. There are some flowers that arrived for you this morning with Mr. Dexter's compliments. They have been placed in the hall.'

'For me!' she blushed, and her horn-rimmed spectacles slipped towards the tip of her nose. 'But why, I wonder?'

'Not on account of your pulchritude; of that you can be sure, Miss Frayle. Mr. Dexter is a good fellow, I should imagine, with a developed sense of humour, and more than a touch of magnanimity. No doubt he is turning the other cheek.'

Miss Frayle said, half to herself: 'The first time I've had flowers from a man, and only because I called him a murderer!'

And with a heavy sigh she picked up her notebook for more of Doctor Morelle's inevitable dictation.

3

The case of the Jeep Driver

Doctor Morelle in the course of his busy life carried out many and various duties, all of which, in spite of his frequently sarcastic tongue, actually gave him a good deal of satisfaction.

It is, however, highly probable that of all the duties which fell to him to perform that which he most enjoyed was the lectures which he occasionally gave to parties of students in the great teaching hospitals of London and the main provincial cities.

He was so well-known for his researches into some of the more obscure recesses of psychology that he was much in demand as a clear and easily understandable lecturer on these difficult problems, One day he was returning from a hospital well on the north side of London, where he had been delivering a lecture on aspects of the subconscious. Miss Frayle was with him, and the Doctor was driving. He was on this occasion very pleased with himself, since the audience had been highly appreciative (Miss Frayle remarked, possibly with a hint of sarcasm, 'Everyone knows that your audiences are *always* appreciative, Doctor,') and at the same time it had been clear, by the nature of the questions that they put at the close of the lecture, that his attitude towards the problems involved had been thoroughly shared by the majority of his listeners.

It was, as a consequence, a completely satisfied Doctor Morelle who sat back in his car and speeded along a lonely stretch of road on the London side of Barnet. Miss Frayle was sitting back and drinking in the air, though now and then she felt more than a twinge of nervousness as they swung around more than one corner at a speed too great to be quite a hundred per cent safe.

Still, in his driving as in other things, the Doctor would not have it that he was anything but efficient. There was, indeed, an air of quiet efficiency about the way in which he grasped the steering wheel, and his general management of the powerful car left nothing to be desired.

Suddenly, however, he leaned forward in his seat and peered intently at the road ahead. Then, with a screaming of brakes, the powerful car, which had been travelling at a speed nearer sixty than fifty miles an hour, came to a standstill.

'Oh, dear, what is it, Doctor?' gasped Miss Frayle, with her hand on her heart.

'I should have thought that it would be obvious even to a person with your chronic lack of perception that a police constable has made his appearance in the exact centre of the road immediately ahead of us,' answered Doctor Morelle.

'I expect that he wants us to stop, you know,' Miss Frayle commented, having by now quite recovered her equilibrium.

'I didn't imagine, Miss Frayle,' answered the Doctor, 'that he was waving his arms in that manner merely to give himself some doubtless beneficial exercise.'

'I do hope,' said Miss Frayle, 'that you aren't going to be pinched for speeding. After all, we were doing nearly sixty miles an hour, weren't we?'

'Surely Miss Frayle,' remarked the Doctor irritably, 'you are aware that this is an open road, and that there are no speed limits in these days, save in those areas which are referred to by the Ministry of Transport as 'built-up'.'

By this time the policeman had approached their car, and was looking through the window, beside the doctor.

'Sorry to stop you, sir,' he said respectfully.

'What is the trouble, constable?' the Doctor asked.

'There's been a bit of an accident nearby, and I want to get hold of a Doctor. There's no 'phone-box for miles, and it would take me a long time to get to it, so I thought that perhaps you would be so good as to . . . '

'You've come to the right shop, officer,' Miss Frayle said, with a chuckle.

'I am Doctor Morelle,' announced the doctor in his most impressive tones.

'That's a lucky break,' said the constable.

'I sincerely hope that such may prove

to be the case,' Doctor Morelle said. 'But can you tell us, Constable, the precise location of the accident to which you were drawing our attention?'

'It's a chap up that turning just along there,' the policeman said, indicating a side road that branched off about fifty yards away. 'Not that there is much that you can do for the poor fellow, I'm afraid.'

'Doesn't seen to have much of an opinion of you, does he, Doctor?' Miss Frayle murmured in Doctor Morelle's ear. 'Perhaps he didn't catch your name.' She leaned over towards the policeman and said, loudly: 'This is Doctor Morelle.'

The policeman sniffed loudly. 'Never 'eard of him,' he said in somewhat supercilious tones, almost worthy of the Doctor himself.

'Oh, dear,' commented Miss Frayle with a sigh. 'I am Miss Frayle,' she explained. The constable looked quite impressed at this revelation. 'Oh yes, I know,' he said. 'You are the young lady who's always getting mixed up with crime and whatnot. Now, what was that last business that I heard about on the wireless the other night?'

Doctor Morelle began to lose patience at the tendency of the conversation to stray.

'Might I suggest,' he said, 'that, before yon start exchanging these doubtless entertaining reminiscences on past events, you give me the opportunity of examining the unfortunate victim of the accident to which you were drawing our attention?'

The constable seemed to be recalled to his sense of duty by this rebuke.

'Of course, Doctor,' he said in rather abashed tones. 'If you like, I'll hop in and I'll direct you to where the body is. It's the first turning to the right, just along there.'

Doctor Morelle started the car as soon as the constable had got in, and Miss Frayle suddenly drew in her breath as the implications of the last remark became clear to her.

'Did you say, 'the body', officer?' she asked, 'Do you mean that the poor man is . . . ' She paused, as if she was unable to utter the word.

'Yes, Miss,' he answered solemnly, 'It looks as if he was murdered, in fact.'

'Oh!' Miss Frayle's hand went to her mouth, and her face grew quite pale, Doctor Morelle was not impressed by this display of emotion. He calmly drove the car to the spot indicated by the policeman, and then drew it to a standstill alongside the vehicle that the constable pointed out.

'Here we are, Doctor,' announced the policeman quietly. 'The poor devil is over in this jeep.'

'One of the vehicles brought to this country by the American Army during the war,' said the Doctor quietly.

'They're called jeeps, Doctor,' Miss Frayle explained in patient tones.

'Thank you, Miss Frayle,' Doctor Morelle answered. 'I was already acquainted with that singularly unharmonious word.'

'Who's that man by the gate?' Miss Frayle asked, indicating a tall, thin individual, standing by a gate about ten yards away from them

'He was with this chap when it happened,' explained the policeman.

Doctor Morelle was not, apparently, listening, for he had got out of his car, and was now making a quick examination of the man in the jeep.

'Dead all right, isn't he, Doctor?' asked the policeman.

'Yes,' said Doctor Morelle. 'Bullet wound over right ear. Life completely extinct. Death instantaneous.' The Doctor turned to the policeman. 'Your earlier prognostication, officer, that there was nothing which I could do for the poor fellow, appears to be perfectly correct.'

'Eh?' said the constable, as if this string of long words were difficult for him to follow. Then he realised the meaning of what had been said. 'Oh, yes, I see what you mean, Doctor,' he added hurriedly.

'What a dreadful thing to happen on this peaceful road!' Miss Frayle exclaimed.

'Have you any idea of how this happened?' Doctor Morelle inquired.

'This other chap will explain,' the constable said. 'He was here when it happened.' He whistled, but the man paid no attention. 'Hi! You're wanted!' shouted the constable. The man started suddenly, and then made his way in their direction.

The man came over. 'You're a doctor, aren't you?' he said in sonorous tones.

'That's right,' said the constable. 'I stopped the first car to come along, and it was a lucky thing that it was a Doctor who was driving it.'

'Nothing you can do for the poor chap, is there?' asked the man.

Doctor Morelle shook his head slowly. 'Nothing at all, I'm afraid,' he said.

'Tell us exactly what happened, will you?' said the policeman.

'Well, you see,' explained the man, 'my pal and I work for Owen and Company — they're the engineering firm, who are putting up that big new factory a couple of miles from here. It'll be a big job when it's finished. Factory for making electrical components, it is. Nearly three hundred on the pay-roll of the construction job, and when the place is built they reckon that it will employ nearly two thousand people.'

'I know the place you mean,' said the policeman, 'A government scheme, isn't it?'

'Yes,' said the man. 'One of these schemes for making employment in a district where there's plenty of labour but not much in the way of big factories to employ them. You know the sort of thing I mean.'

'And you were working for this organisation,' Doctor Morelle said.

'Yes. My pal and I were on our way from the head office in London in this old jeep with this week's wages. We come along every Friday with it.'

'Must have been a pretty tidy sum,' commented the policeman, 'if you have three hundred people on the payroll.'

'Between two and three thousand quid,' the man agreed. 'It was packed in three boxes.'

'All that as usual?' the constable asked.

'Yes. It happened every week, and had done for months past. Well, we'd turned into this lane, and two soldiers thumbed us for a lift. My mate was driving, and I thought that it was a dangerous business with all that cash on board, so I told him not to stop.'

'But he did stop,' said Miss Frayle,

more in the nature of someone taking a statement than of someone asking a question.

'He did, Miss,' agreed the man. 'He didn't think that it would do any harm. As he stopped one of the chaps came up to him, suddenly waved a gun in his face, and told him to put his hands up. My mate started to say something — I think that he was going to argue with them — and I yelled at him to step on it quick. But before he could do a thing about it, this soldier let him have it with the gun.'

Again Miss Frayle showed her usual emotional reaction to such a story of violent events.

'How ghastly!' she exclaimed.

'Yes, Miss,' the man agreed. 'Poor old Fred slumped over the wheel like he is now. The soldier waved his gun at me in a threatening sort of way, and said that if I didn't want a dose of the same medicine as he had had, I should have to do as I was told, and do it quick.'

'And what did he ask you to do?' inquired the policeman.

'He leaned across old Fred and kept his

gun pointed at me while his pal took the three boxes of money out of the back of the jeep. They wheeled a motorbike and sidecar from the side of the road, dumped the boxes of money into it, and off they went. The bike had been more or less hidden in the hedge over there.' The man indicated a spot only a few yards distant.

Doctor Morelle had listened intently to this recital of the facts, but had made no comment up to now. It seemed, however, that he had decided that it was now time for him to intervene.

'You, of course, made no effort to prevent them from making good their escape?' he said.

The man shrugged his shoulders expressively. 'How could I?' he asked. 'What good could I have done? I'd seen enough to know what would happen to me if I tried on any funny business. I'd have had it as well, and they'd still have got away with it. And there would have been nobody left to tell the tale — which would have meant that there would have been mighty little chance of anybody ever finding out what had happened. I reckoned that if I kept quiet I should save my own life, and maybe be able to do something to help to catch the devils.'

'Of course,' murmured Miss Frayle.

'I am quite sure,' Doctor Morelle said, 'that you acted very prudently.'

'Then, after they'd got away,' the policeman added, 'this chap ran up the main road and I came on the scene. It was a lucky thing that I happened to be passing just at the moment. Otherwise it might have been hours before you got hold of anybody who was able to do anything about the business.'

Doctor Morelle was looking slightly puzzled about something, and Miss Frayle recognised the symptoms. But just what it was that was puzzling him she found it extremely difficult to understand. Even after her long experience of the Doctor's ways, she still found it difficult to follow the way in which his mind worked. She often said, indeed, that his brain was a machine, the working of which she was totally unable to appreciate.

'You left the deceased in the vehicle

here?' the Doctor said suddenly after a momentary silence.

'Yes.'

The Doctor was clearly not at all satisfied. 'Surely,' he said, 'it would have been quicker had you driven the vehicle out on to the main road?'

'You're telling me,' replied the man with a surly grin. 'The only thing is, I can't drive.'

Doctor Morelle digested the information in silence. It appeared that he was satisfied, at any rate for the moment, and the slight frown of bewilderment that had appeared on his forehead had now disappeared. Miss Frayle was puzzled at his reactions, since she could not see that this last snatch of conversation had really cleared up anything.

The constable, apparently a trifle put out by the way in which the Doctor had taken on the initiative in cross-examination, now resumed his questioning.

'Could you identify the two soldiers if you saw them again, do you think?' he asked.

'I'm pretty sure I could,' replied the

man in decided tones. 'Of course, you've got to remember that a chap in uniform looks a bit different from what he does in civvies.'

'Was there anything about their faces that you can remember them by?' asked the constable.

'The fellow with the gun — the chap that shot poor old Fred — had a front tooth missing, I remember noticing. He had a very red face, too. As for the other chap . . . ' He paused for a moment, and then went on: 'Well, I don't know that there was much about him to distinguish him. He was a very ordinary-looking chap. Nothing special about him.'

Doctor Morelle now took up the questioning again. 'Were you able to distinguish to which branches of the Amy the two men in question belonged?' he asked.

The man hesitated. 'No; I'm a bit hazy about that, I'm afraid,' he admitted. 'As a matter of fact, I don't think that they had any shoulder flashes or anything of that sort.'

Miss Frayle looked up brightly at the

man. 'Perhaps they weren't soldiers at all,' she suggested. 'They may have got hold of the uniforms from somewhere and decided that it would be a good scheme to use them as a sort of disguise.'

'That's a good idea, Miss,' said the constable, looking at her with a glance of something very like admiration.

'I do get them sometimes, don't I, Doctor?' Miss Frayle said, looking mischievously at Doctor Morelle.

Doctor Morelle did not echo the constable's admiration. 'My dear Miss Frayle,' he said in his most sardonic tones, 'the possibility that you have suggested occurred to me several minutes ago.'

'Oh,' said Miss Frayle, somewhat taken aback by this response to what she thought was a brilliant idea.

'Oh,' echoed the constable, who was equally surprised that Miss Frayle suggestion had so completely failed to impress the Doctor.

Doctor Morelle, on the other hand, was in no way disconcerted at this reaction to his remarks. He was, of course, quite accustomed to his statements causing a certain amount of alarm or even despondency among those who listened to him. He now turned to the man again.

'The gun you say the soldier used with which to kill your companion and to threaten yourself,' he said. 'Did you manage to observe what type it was?'

The man grinned sourly, 'Big, ugly-looking job it was,' he said. 'It looked to me like an Army one — though, of course, I may have been led to think that because the men were in uniform.'

'When did you first notice the presence of the two men?' asked Doctor Morelle.

'Oh, they must have been about fifty yards or so ahead of us when I saw them first,' replied the man. 'I saw 'em standing at the side of the road. Sort of lurking, they were, rather as if they didn't want to be seen.'

'Did you get the impression, then, that they were lying in wait for you?' the Doctor asked.

'No, not for us especially, although that was what they were trying to do all right. But they just looked a little bit suspicious, if you know what I mean.'

It was clear that Doctor Morelle did *not* know what this meant, as his sniff of faint derision at once suggested. The constable, not sensitive to the moods of Doctor Morelle, did not realise what the Doctor was thinking, and remarked: 'They must have found out that you were carrying all that pay money, and . . . '

Doctor Morelle, pursuing a train of thought of his own, broke in impatiently with the further question: 'Which side of the road were they standing?'

'Nearside, of course,' replied the man without any hesitation.

'They wouldn't be waiting on the other side unless they wanted to stop a car coming the other way,' Miss Frayle remarked with an air of triumph.

'That's right, Miss,' agreed the constable, staunchly loyal to a lady whom he clearly thought a paragon of clear thinking.

Doctor Morelle, however, rounded on her savagely. 'I wonder, my dear Miss Frayle,' he remarked in his most icily sarcastic tones, 'if I might prevail on you occasionally to refrain from uttering such completely aimless banalities?'

Miss Frayle pouted slightly, 'I was only trying to help, Doctor,' she said.

'I must say,' remarked the policemen, 'That *I* thought that was quite a bright suggestion of its kind.'

'Thank you, Sergeant,' smiled Miss Frayle.

'Constable, Miss, as yet, though, of course, I have my hopes for the future,' he replied, smiling at her in his turn, to the obvious disgust of Doctor Morelle.

Miss Frayle grasped his arm suddenly. 'Look!' she exclaimed. 'Here's a cyclist coming up the road. He might be able to help. After all, it's quite possible that he saw the man's motor bike.'

'We'll stop him and see if he can tell us anything,' the constable announced.

The dead man's companion seemed to be a trifle taken aback by this. 'Of course, there are two or three side turnings that they might have dodged down,' he pointed out, As the cyclist approached the constable said: 'I say, excuse me. Have you seen a couple of chaps with a motor bike and sidecar pass you?'

'Eh?' asked the man, cupping his hand around his ear and dismounting.

'Sorry to stop you,' said Miss Frayle, 'but there has been a murder.'

'Eh?' said the man again, looking at them in a mystified manner.

'He must be deaf,' commented Miss Frayle.

'None so deaf as those that don't want to hear,' said the constable sententiously.

Miss Frayle realised that it was time that someone did something to make the cyclist see what had happened. So she shouted at the top of her voice.

'Have two men on a motor bike passed you recently?' she fairly yelled.

'Eh?' said the cyclist for the third time. 'What's the matter? I don't understand at all! What's going on here?' And, indeed, the man looked completely bewildered, as if the whole affair was quite beyond him. Doctor Morelle realised that these people would merely continue to make the matter more complex, no matter what they did. It was high time, he thought, that he once more took control of the situation. And on this occasion, at any rate, there was little doubt that Doctor Morelle's healthy self-conceit was justified up to the hilt, even though neither Miss Frayle nor the constable would have been prepared to admit such a thing at the time. One of the most irritating things about Doctor Morelle was that his air of conscious superiority was almost invariably justified. His friends found this difficult to endure, and this was one of the occasions when Miss Frayle found him most difficult. Yet he achieved his end, as usual, not by shouting or raging, but by being quietly efficient.

'Perhaps,' he said quietly, 'I might be permitted to address this gentleman for a moment. I think that I could discover the fact of the matter.'

'Poor man,' said Miss Frayle in sympathetic tones, 'I'm afraid he is very deaf.'

Doctor Morelle returned to the man and spoke to him in ordinary conversational tones, but speaking slowly and with great distinctness, marking off each word separately.

'I should like to know,' he said, 'if, on your way here, you encountered a motor bike and sidecar with two men who were attired as soldiers.'

The man smiled cheerfully. 'Ah, that's better,' he said. 'Why couldn't the others speak properly? I couldn't make head or tail of their muttering.'

Miss Frayle gave vent to a sound that in anyone else would have been definitely classified as a snort.

'Two men dressed as soldiers, riding on a motor bike with a sidecar?' the cyclist repeated. He shook his head decisively. 'No, sir,' he went on. 'I certainly don't remember meeting them on the road, and I've been coming along slow and steady like.'

Doctor Morelle turned to the constable. 'Are there any further questions which you would like to ask this man?' he asked.

'I don't think so, Doctor,' the constable replied.

'Good!' Doctor Morelle said, rubbing his hands briskly together, 'and, in that case I think that you can now safely detain your suspect.'

'What!' exclaimed the constable. 'Suspect? Who do you think is the suspect in this?'

Miss Frayle burst in on this puzzled speech with a sudden shout.

'Doctor Morelle!' she almost screamed. 'Quick, the man's going off on his bike!'

The constable was now galvanised into activity. 'Hi, you!' he shouted, breaking into a run. 'Come back at once! Where do you think you're going?'

'You'll have to hurry,' said the murdered man's companion with a grin. 'He's deaf, you know. He won't hear a word that you say.'

The constable now fairly raced down the road in the wake of the fast-disappearing cycle. Miss Frayle was unable to resist a chuckle at the sight of the ponderous policeman lumbering along the road, and Doctor Morelle regarded the whole proceedings with a disapproving frown.

★ ★ ★

The whole matter was, however, cleared up to Miss Frayle's satisfaction that evening, when, in the Doctor's study, she had the job of getting down on paper a description of the case, to be included in the voluminous notes on criminology which Doctor Morelle was compiling, partly for the purpose of making up his casebooks and partly to take their place in an enormous encyclopedia of crime which he aimed to write sometime in the rather indefinite future.

'The whole business is a most complete puzzle to me, I must admit,' she said, as the Doctor concluded his description of the way in which they had been called in to investigate the curious case of the man in the jeep.

'I did not expect, my dear Miss Frayle, that the matter would be clear to a person with your particular kind of intellect — if that is the correct word to describe the process which goes on inside your skull,' the Doctor said. 'But if you will kindly force yourself to exert what abilities you have in getting down in shorthand my description of the way in which I arrived at my inevitable conclusions, you will find that the matter, as far as your own mind is concerned, will swiftly clarify itself.'

Miss Frayle was in no way abashed at this slight on her mental ability. She had now worked for the Doctor for such a long time that she was accustomed to having sarcastic shafts of wit aimed at her from all angles.

'The cyclist of course,' the Doctor went on, 'was in no way incriminated. He was exceedingly deaf.'

'Then how was it,' asked Miss Frnyle, 'that he could not hear me when I positively shrieked at him, but could hear you, though you spoke to him in quite ordinary tones?'

'His ability to hear me when I addressed him,' the Doctor explained, 'was due to the fact that I purposely faced him directly and spoke very clearly and distinctly. Then, as so many deaf persons do, consciously or unconsciously, he was lip-reading. In other words, he did not *listen* to me at all; he just followed what my lips were saying.'

Miss Frayle looked duly impressed at

this revelation. 'And I thought,' she said pensively, 'that it was because you had such an especially penetrating voice.'

Doctor Morelle looked — as if such a thing were possible — rather more irritated than was his wont.

'Do concentrate less on your own wild and foolish imaginings,' he snapped, 'and a little more upon your notebook, which is the inscrutable process by which my reasoning will be made available for posterity.'

'Do you really mean that, Doctor?' Miss Frayle asked, for once impressed in spite of herself.

'I do,' the Doctor replied, 'and when I have concluded this not unimportant chapter for my casebook, I will demonstrate to you my method of making deaf people comprehend what I am saying without putting myself under the necessity of screeching my head off.'

'Oh, Doctor,' said Miss Frayle, 'I can hardly wait for that to happen.'

The Doctor heaved a sigh. He gave the impression that he was sorely tried by the way in which his secretary failed to appreciate the superlative manner in which he had conducted his case.

'Let us proceed, then,' he said.

'Certainly,' responded Miss Frayle, and poised her pencil expectantly.

'The deceased's companion,' Doctor Morelle went on, 'the man who described in such graphic detail how the vehicle had been held up by two mysterious individuals attired as soldiers, and how the driver had been shot, was himself the murderer.'

Miss Frayle now found herself impelled to admire the amazing working of the Doctor's mind.

'I don't know how you do it, Doctor,' she exclaimed. 'To me that man's story sounded completely convincing.'

'To a person of your intellectual equipment,' responded Doctor Morelle, 'it would doubtless so appear. To me the fact that the bullet wound was above the driver's right ear at once disproved his companion's statement, which he had concocted, in order, as he thought, to shield himself from all possible suspicion. Had I not been present he would doubtless have succeeded in persuading the other witnesses of the complete innocence of his motives.'

A puzzled frown was wrinkling Miss Frayle's brow. 'I still don't see . . . ' she began.

'What do you not see?' asked the Doctor querulously.

'I don't see that the position of the bullet wound proves anything at all about the man's guilt or innocence of the crime in which the driver was killed.'

Doctor Morelle grunted, 'The American Army motor vehicle known, I believe as a cheep . . . '

Miss Frayle interrupted him, 'Jeep, Doctor Morelle, Jeep,' she said.

'Pray refrain, Miss Frayle,' he said, 'from chirping at me like a linnet or some other species of bird.'

Miss Frayle smiled to herself, but said nothing.

'As I was saying,' the Doctor went on sedately, 'the American Army vehicle known as a jeep has a left-hand drive, which is to say that the driver sits on the left-hand side of the front seat when he steers the vehicle.'

'I have heard of a left-hand drive, Doctor,' Miss Frayle pointed out.

'You surprise me, Miss Frayle,' answered Doctor Morelle. 'But you do not appear to realise the implications of the left-hand drive of the jeep in the present instance. The main point is that anyone approaching close to the driver on the nearside and shooting him in the head, in the way described by the dead man's companion, would inflict a bullet wound on the *left* side. It would indeed have been totally impossible had the man's story been true in detail for the bullet to have entered the driver's head at the point it did. As he later confessed, the murderer had himself shot the driver from his position on the seat beside him, and had hidden the money and murder weapon in a nearby ditch with the object of subsequently returning and recovering it. Three thousand pounds is an adequate motive for a murder.'

'I'm afraid,' said Miss Frayle, chuckling quickly, 'that I didn't quite get down that last part, Doctor. You see, I get so carried away by the brilliance of your logical deductions that sometimes I quite forget to pay due attention to my shorthand and don't get everything written down.'

Doctor Morelle looked more irritated than ever. 'Do try to pull yourself together, Miss Frayle,' he said. 'I have come to a conclusion which I trust may cause you some gratification.'

'What is that, Doctor?' Miss Frayle asked.

'I have decided that I am going to dedicate my next casebook to you.'

'Oh, thank you, Doctor Morelle. How very sweet of you.'

Miss Frayle was, indeed, highly flattered at the thought, though her pleasure was somewhat marred by the remarks that followed.

'The dedication will go like this: 'To my dear Miss Frayle, but for whose helpful co-operation this book would have been completed in half the time'.'

Not for the first time, Miss Frayle was speechless — and not with pleasure.

4

The case of the man Overboard

'Muster for lifeboat drill — 'A' deck!'

Miss Frayle thrilled as she heard a steward calling out those words. She turned from the porthole where, bright-eyed, she had been watching the sea surging below, and she thought: 'Who would have imagined a week ago that here I'd be on a mammoth Atlantic liner, bound for New York — it's so exciting.' She reached for the lifesaving impedi-menta that were hung neatly behind the cabin door.

Doctor Morelle had been invited to attend a conference of worldwide scien-tific importance in New York. As the invitation was, very naturally, most pressing, he had sailed, accompanied by Miss Frayle, on the liner *Georgie*. It had been a hectic time for Miss Frayle, rushing through the passport formalities, and packing all the luggage for the trip. However, in her anticipation of the sea voyage, and several weeks in the New World, she had tackled the task with feverish energy and joyful anticipation.

And here they were, on the first day drawing out of the Channel into the wide Atlantic. In a day or two they would be in the Gulf Stream, and they would see porpoises, and maybe even whales. Then there would be the landing, and her first glimpse of the New York skyscrapers, and all the reporters interviewing Doctor Morelle, and perhaps even taking photographs of her.

She stretched her arms luxuriously. 'How lucky I am,' she rhapsodised. 'Thousands of women would envy me.'

She did not even dread seasickness because she had taken the precaution of procuring every known remedy, and these, though probably not physically efficacious, gave her great confidence. She had plasticine earplugs; a patent body-belt; capsules and diagrammatical charts showing exactly how one should lie face downwards in the bunk. The Doctor scornfully pooh-poohed all these precautions, but Miss Frayle was determined not to suffer from *mal-de-mer* — if only to triumph for once over him.

'Muster for Lifeboat drill . . . ' The steward's cry came from further down the corridor.

She grabbed the apparatus, and, slipping the long brass hook off the door, ran towards the Doctor's cabin round the corner.

He had already fixed on his lifebelt and was tightening the last strap.

'Wait for me, Doctor Morelle,' she exclaimed. 'It won't take me a minute.'

She slipped a strap over her head, and contorted herself to fasten it. He watched her sardonically.

'How singularly inefficient you are, my dear Miss Frayle,' he said softly. 'Should an emergency arise, you would no doubt dislocate your collar-bone preparatory to drowning.'

'I can't — can't get this to reach across,' she gasped. 'It doesn't seem long enough.' She contorted herself in a knot. 'Does — does this go at the front or back?'

He leaned against the cabin door, a mocking smile on his lips as he drew at a Le Sphinx.

'Oh, why don't you help me instead of standing there smirking?' she burst out.

'Really, Miss Frayle, if I affixed the life-preserving apparatus for you, the effect of this drill would be nullified. The object of the muster is to enable you to learn how to accomplish it for yourself.' He tapped the ash off his cigarette, 'To anyone of normal intelligence, the affixing of the lifebelt is simplicity itself. Hurry, our presence is essential on Deck 'A'!'

Completely oblivious of her discomfiture, he walked out of the cabin with long raking strides, and she followed, wrestling with the apparatus. She tried to see how he had fixed his, and it seemed entirely different from hers. Well, no doubt one of the ship's officers would be more obliging and would show her exactly how it should be done.

Other people were already lining up on the deck. The muster was voluntary, but most of the passengers seemed to be there. Breathlessly Miss Frayle took her place in the line, next to the Doctor. A clear-eyed young officer was walking smartly down the file, inspecting the lifebelts strapped to each passenger. He paused in front of Miss Frayle, scrutinising her apparatus, and then looked her directly in the eyes. Of course she had got it all wrong, she thought — thanks to the Doctor! If only he hadn't hurried her. She flushed with shame.

'May I ask your name, please?' the young officer asked politely.

'M-M-Miss Frayle,' she stammered. This was dreadful!

'Would you mind stepping forward, Miss Frayle?' the officer requested courteously.

She hesitated, and glanced up at the Doctor, hoping futilely that he would rescue her or make some excuse for her — anything!

A sardonic smile quirked his thin lips, and she knew that she would get nothing but sneers from him.

'Hurry, Miss Frayle,' he snapped. 'The officer is waiting.'

Dreading every second, fearing she was

to be made to look foolish, stupid and inefficient in front of all the other passengers, she stumbled forward three paces across the deck, She felt like a pirate walking the plank.

The officer inspected her with smiling friendliness, and then turned to the other passengers.

'Would you please gather round Miss Frayle. Many of you, I am afraid, have made minor mistakes in the affixing of your apparatus, but this young lady — ' he grinned at her charmingly, 'this young lady has correctly fixed her lifebelt, completely in accordance with the regulations. By observing Miss Frayle's belt you will see how it should be fixed.'

She had done it correctly! And she was the only one! Miss Frayle glowed with pride. She held her head high. Pointedly, she flashed a glance to the Doctor. He appeared to be pretending that he was not aware of what was happening.

'Thank you, Miss Frayle,' the officer was saying.

'Thank you. Oh, thank you!' she

gasped in sincere gratitude. Her happiness was complete when she noticed another officer standing by Doctor Morelle and altering the straps, politely explaining to the bored Doctor exactly how it should have been done. Miss Frayle delightedly allowed her kit to be examined by other passengers. As she walked back to their cabins with the Doctor, she could not refrain from saying:

'You were quite right, Doctor. It was simplicity itself to anyone of normal intelligence!'

It may well be imagined he was not in the best of humours when Miss Frayle later tapped at his door, and, with irritating brightness, summoned him for the first luncheon. He strode down the deck beside her, an expression of boredom on his face. But his blasé manner did not have a dampening effect on her high spirits. She was thrilled by everything, from the swimming pool to the shops on board; the gymnasium and the kennels with the pedigree dogs barking at her in their pens. Even the Doctor's laconic and half-derisive manner was not going to detract from the pleasure of her voyage.

They passed through the open doorway into the dining room. An orchestra behind some palms was playing one of the less sentimental Strauss waltzes, and Miss Frayle's eyes were dreamy, until she heard a middle-aged feminine voice shrilling flamboyantly:

'Why, it's Doctor Morelle — of all people!'

They turned round to observe a dumpy, over-dressed woman, who was hurrying towards them with an ostentatiously outstretched hand.

Doctor Morelle returned the gushing smile with a look of blank inquiry.

'Now don't say you've forgotten me, or I guess I'll just curl up and die,' the woman mouéd. She looked at him archly, her eyes sparkling in her over-cosmeticised face. An absurd kiss-curl dangled from her elaborately coiffured head.

'It was at the American Embassy in Paris about six years ago,' she exclaimed. 'Surely you remember Mrs. Van der Husen?'

'I fear I do not recollect the name,' he murmured icily.

'Maybe I was Lady Singleton then — or Mrs. Trotter?' she hazarded helpfully.

'Ah, a lady of many aliases!'

'Not aliases — you wicked man!' she said skittishly. 'Merely marriages. I rather lose track myself — let me see, there was Bertie, Freddie and Dunks — he was the last one. Oh, I guess I've been round the world three times since I last saw you, Doctor. Each trip I get five years younger. But, of course, you wouldn't know me now.' She gave a hint of a wink to the astonished Miss Frayle. 'My hair was *red* in those days!'

Teasingly she tapped Doctor Morelle on the arm and asked meaningfully:

'And who is the young lady?'

He coughed. His voice was scarcely audible as he introduced them:

'Mrs. Van der Husen — Miss Frayle, my assistant.'

'Assistant!' The woman shrilled. 'Well, if that ain't a honey — !' she broke off as she sensed the intense chill in the

Doctor's manner. 'Now there I go again saying the wrong thing. Bertie always used to say to me: 'Mary, you'll waggle that tongue of yours once too often and someday someone will murder you'!' She gave a peal of strident laughter. 'Imagine anyone wanting to murder little me!'

Doctor Morelle was edging away from her. 'I fear, madam, we are detaining you. Good evening — '

'No — you don't, Doctor! You're not going to escape like that!' she declared, and she threaded a bejewelled hand through his arm. 'You're taking me in to lunch.' She led him towards the Captain's table. 'The very moment I came aboard I looked through the passengers' list — to see if there were any celebrities — any friends of mine, and when I saw your name I insisted the Captain sat you next to me.' She caught Miss Frayle's hand warmly. 'I've ordered them to put a magnum of champagne on ice to celebrate the reunion, dear. I must find you a nice young man — then I'll be able to have the Doctor all to myself!'

During the lunch, Doctor Morelle

merely spoke m monosyllables. Several times Captain Kenrick gave him a sympathetic glance, as though he felt sorry for his being saddled with such a loquacious and possessive companion.

Mrs Van der Husen, it seemed, had spent most of her parasitic life travelling from Gleneagles to Paris, from Berlin to Biarritz, Mentone to Le Touquet; and her hobby was collecting celebrities and husbands. Her homes were the luxury hotels of the world. She was an alimony wife of the worst type; she had neither good looks nor natural wit. Her conversation, it is true, had a certain ebullient quality because of the quite slanderous, first-hand tales she had collected concerning notabilities on whom she had inflicted herself. To the Doctor, who was quite above international intrigue and social tittle-tattle, she was merely prolonged and unadulterated tedium.

After ascertaining that Mrs. Van der Husen would be attending the first dinner, the Doctor abruptly returned to his cabin and briskly informed Miss Frayle that he would be dining at the second session. She heard him locking and bolting his cabin, as though for added protection against the ubiquitous and unsnubbable divorcee.

Fortunately Mrs. Van der Husen was not in the dining room when the gong for the second session was sounded, and Miss Frayle deduced — and hoped — she had found some other lion who was more tameable than the irascible Doctor.

It was when he was applying his lighter to the inevitable Le Sphinx, while coffee was being served, that a woman's piercing shriek sounded from the A-deck doorway, and Mrs. Van der Husen ran into the dining room, babbling and screaming incoherently. The orchestra stopped playing. Captain Kenrick rose to his feet with a wearied expression.

'Man overboard! Port side of A deck,' screamed Mrs. Van der Husen. 'I saw it all! It — it was murder!'

She stumbled across to Doctor Morelle, her eyes starting out of her painted face.

'I was looking for you, Doctor Morelle,' she explained excitedly. 'I thought we might take a turn on the deck. It's dark out there. I got chilled — I was coming back — and then — then I saw it happen — ' She shuddered dramatically, and placed her hands over her eyes. In a hushed, theatrical tone she continued. 'A man was leaning against the rail. A second later another man came up behind him, walking softly. I thought he was going to play a joke or something. Then the second man stepped behind the first one, hit him over the head with something, and lifted him overboard. I saw — saw him fall into that black water! It was — *horrible!*'

Captain Kennick urgently rose to his feet and left the dining room. A few minutes later the passengers in the dining room heard the giant screws slow down. The ship ceased its vibrating.

'What do you make of it, Doctor?' Miss Frayle questioned anxiously. 'Do you think Mrs. Van der Husen really did see — ?'

'I believe this will be extremely fortuitous,' he replied laconically. 'Mrs. Van der Husen is obviously psychopathologically exhibitionistic. No doubt she found herself to be deservedly neglected during dinner, and has planned this ruse to attract attention to herself. Should such be the case we shall be secure against her unwelcome attentions — but I rather fear that the Master-at-arms is going to have a most troublesome prisoner!'

'I hope they put her in chains, alarming everyone like this,' Miss Frayle said indignantly. 'Why, they've stopped the engines.'

'Your perspicacity continues to amaze me, my dear Miss Frayle,' he snapped, and he sat down to drink his coffee. Half an hour later the Captain returned, and informed the passengers that he had ordered his officers to request everyone to return to the cabins, in order that the stewards might conduct a roll-call of the passengers.

An hour later, when the roll-call was finished, Mrs. Van der Husen burst into Miss Frayle's cabin, her eyes agog with some dynamic news that she was anxious to impart.

'I was the only one who saw the

murder, Miss Frayle,' she babbled. 'I've just been telling the master-at-Arms all about it. Of course, it was very dark and I couldn't give a very *exact* description of the man who did it.'

'I often think,' observed Miss Frayle coldly, 'that one often hears strange sounds in a ship, and shadows on the deck are sometimes very misleading too.' She looked the other straight in the eyes. 'Are you sure you did not imagine it, Mrs. Van der Husen?'

'Imagine it! Don't talk such rubbish, girl! Imagine it, indeed! I've never heard of such a thing.' She fluffed up her baby curls indignantly. 'If I had imagined it — which I didn't — how do you account for the fact that there is a passenger missing?'

'Someone missing!' echoed Miss Frayle, a hand fluttering to her throat in agitation. 'You mean someone fell into the water and they haven't recovered him?'

'They searched round — and found nothing.' Mrs. Van der Husen paused with horrible gloating. 'The man was probably ripped to pieces by the propeller

— and the Master-at-Arms said it was jolly good riddance!'

'But how horribly brutal. What — what did he mean?'

'The man who is missing was a terrible man.' Mrs. Van der Husen fluttered her eyelids. 'He preyed on people like — like a vampire. He was a blackmailer. The ship's detectives knew all about him. They had their eyes on him as soon as he stepped aboard. His name was — Lawrence Devereux — '

Miss Frayle stood against the light, her jaw dropped and her mouth forming a shocked O.

'I suppose he would worm secrets out of people and then he'd — ?'

'Yes, he'd bleed them white — like a vampire,' nodded Mrs. Van der Husen with a sticky smile. She flopped down on the settee, and patted the place beside her. 'Now you sit down here, and we'll have a nice cosy chat, before that wolf of a Doctor appears. I've got such a lot of things I want to ask you.' Her voice took on a wheedling tone. 'Everyone says that Doctor Morelle is a woman-hater. But I

130

don't believe it. No man is! Now tell me — and I promise I won't breathe a word of it to anyone — tell me, does he — ?'

Miss Frayle stiffened. 'My work for Doctor Morelle is entirely confidential,' she said icily. She pressed a hand to her forehead. 'I'm sorry, Mrs. Van der Husen, I have a headache. I think I'll lie down — '

'You want to get rid of me!' the other exclaimed, leaping up and making for the door. 'I must say you are not very friendly.' Her gaze swept Miss Frayle with nauseating innuendo. 'I suppose you're one of the *deep*, solitary ones.'

As soon as the woman had gone, Miss Frayle stood up clenching her hands tightly, and after powdering her face she went in search of the purser, and asked him if Doctor Morelle and she could have a double table to themselves, instead of having to sit next to Mrs. Van der Husen. Discreetly and sympathetically the purser made the necessary arrangements. Miss Frayle knew the Doctor could not fail to approve her resourcefulness.

She left the purser's office and returned

along the deck. There were lights about, but there were also dark shadows in the corners, and suddenly her footsteps quickened. It seemed as though someone was following her. She shot a glance over her shoulder. Was there someone to the left of that window? Or was it her imagination? A chill fear came over her. Somewhere in the ship was a murderer free to roam about — free to commit another crime. Maybe — maybe he was a homicidal maniac. Convinced now there really were creeping footsteps behind her, and two outstretched hands reaching to claw her throat, she broke into a frenzied run and burst breathlessly into the well-lit corridor.

She paused outside her cabin. The door was half open, and yet — yet she had placed it ajar on the long brass hook. Or had she? She tensed her hands trying to pull herself together. She tried to convince herself that her fears were purely imagination. Briskly she entered the cabin and depressed the light switch. The light did not come on, and Miss Frayle gave a strangulated shriek as she saw a huge dim figure looming in the half-darkness of her cabin.

'Who's there?' she squeaked tremulously.

There was a muffled cough. She tried to back to the door as she saw the figure approaching her. The door swung closed behind her.

'Answer m-m-me,' she stammered. 'I — I h-have a l-l-loaded r-r-revolver and I won't h-h-hesitate to shoot!'

She started convulsively as a male voice boomed in her ears.

'Whoever you are,' the voice blared, 'please leave my cabin this instant.'

'*Your* cabin!' she repeated, partly forgetting her panic in her indignation. 'This is my cabin!'

'Yours!' the male voice echoed through the darkness. 'If that is so, then I have made a grievous mistake. Allow me, dear lady.'

The voice was courteous and conciliatory now. She heard the click of a cigarette lighter, and in the flickering flame she saw a tall, middle-aged man with a comforting genial, smiling face. He was dressed reassuringly in earthy tweeds.

'It appears indeed that I have made a mistake,' the man said. 'A thousand apologies, my dear lady.'

'You — you gave me the fright of my life,' she murmured. Then she pointed towards the bed. 'Oh, look! The light bulb's fallen out onto the bed. So that's why the light would not come on.'

Adroitly the man socketed the bulb in position again, and the light came on. The intruder was smiling at her charmingly She noticed his disarming eyes, and his curly brown hair.

'I'm sorry I threatened to shoot you,' she said with a nervous laugh. 'Actually I haven't even got anything as dangerous as a hat pin!'

'It is I who should apologise,' he smiled. 'I returned to what thought was my cabin to retrieve a handkerchief, and I found the light was not working. I presumed the bulb had burnt out and I made a mental note to inform the steward. I then went to the drawer where I imagined I kept my handkerchief.' He indicated the open drawer. 'I fear I have rummaged the contents somewhat.'

'That doesn't matter,' she said brightly. 'It was a natural enough mistake.' Miss Frayle paused. She was imagining herself telling the Doctor about this occurrence — omitting any details of course about her paralytic terror — and to give the story more weight, she decided she ought to ascertain the intruder's identity.

'I don't think we have been introduced, Mr. — er — er,' she hazarded. 'My name is Miss Frayle — '

'How do you do,' the man murmured politely. 'Allow me.' He drew out a card from a waistcoat pocket, and handed it to her. Any lingering suspicions that she might have still entertained were dispelled as she read the name embossed on the strip of pasteboard: *Sir Aubrey Halliday*. He shook her hand in friendliness.

'Now we have been formally introduced, and I trust my intrusion has not caused you undue alarm,' he said politely as he moved to the door.

'I was rather on edge,' she excused herself. 'That murderer — at large and — '

'Shocking business. Most sordid!' he agreed. 'Well, good evening, Miss Frayle.'

'Good evening, Sir Aubrey.'

Next day, after an enjoyable morning playing deck quoits with some of the younger passengers, Miss Frayle joined Doctor Morelle for second lunch. Mrs. Van der Husen glanced across the luncheon room at her balefully from the Captain's table, but she did not as much as incline her head in greeting. Nevertheless she appeared to be eyeing Miss Frayle closely. Doctor Morelle had already been sitting at his table for five minutes, and had postponed ordering until she arrived. He did not hesitate to show his irritation at her tardiness.

Miss Frayle picked up her table-napkin and undid the starchy folds. A piece of paper fluttered from the napkin on to the tablecloth.

'Oh, Doctor Morelle!' she exclaimed. 'Look — a piece of paper's fallen out of my table-napkin!'

He spoke urgently, in an undertone.

'Pass it to me, quickly!'

She turned the folded slip of paper in

her hands speculatively.

'But whatever can it be?' she puzzled.

'Will you cease waving it like a flag, and pass it to me,' he snapped angrily.

'But I must read it,' she protested. She opened the folds. 'How exciting — it's a note and says — Oh!' She broke off, her eyes goggling behind their lenses.

'Give it me — ' exclaimed the Doctor in ill-tempered tones, and he shot out his hand possessively.

'It's very rude to snatch like that!' she pouted. 'After all it is my note — '

'We will discuss both my good manners and this missive elsewhere,' he retorted sharply. 'Come with me.'

'Oh, can't we wait till after lunch?'

'Miss Frayle, kindly adjust your spectacles on your nose correctly before they fall into the soup, making you even more conspicuous than you now appear — '

'I see you want the note to be a secret!' she deduced brightly.

He clicked his tongue impatiently as he pushed back his chair from the table.

'And follow me on deck, where there is a degree of privacy, and I will try to elucidate this little mystery . . . '

'Oh, dear,' she murmured wearily, rising to her feet, 'and I was so looking forward to my lunch.'

'Come along!'

'How do you suppose the note got into my napkin?' she pondered as she followed him through the doorway on to the deck. Studiously he ignored her question. He led her to a corner where they would not be observed.

'Here we are,' he exclaimed. He regarded her with pained displeasure. 'And I do wish, Miss Frayle, you would obey me at once and without question.'

'Well, I only — ' she began.

'Babbling away about this note so that I was forced to still your tongue by bringing you out here,' he rasped. He paused and then went on: 'It's a hoax, without a doubt — I had a similar piece of paper in my table-napkin at breakfast — nevertheless — '

'You never told me,' she said reproachfully.

He raised his eyebrows quizzically.

'I am not aware I am obliged to inform

you how I spend every moment of my day!'

'No, of course not,' she nodded, 'but I think — '

'My communication this morning was in these words,' he interrupted. He drew a slip of paper from a pocket. 'Here, I will read it: '*Keep your eye on Cabin number forty-six*'.'

'Is that all?'

'Precisely.' He examined the note closely. 'Succinct yet intriguing. I deduced the message was from some feckless pseudo-practical joker, and decided to ignore the matter.'

Miss Frayle smiled up at the Doctor with somewhat overdone sweetness.

'And now, Doctor, perhaps you'd be kind enough to read me the other note?' she murmured. 'After all, it was sent to me.'

He examined the second note.

'The paper and writing are the same,' he observed. 'It reads: '*Tell the Doctor to check up on Sir Aubrey Halliday. This is serious*'.'

'Sir Aubrey!' Miss Frayle gasped. 'Why,

that's the man who wandered into my cabin last evening by mistake. He's a charming man — '

'He is also the occupant of cabin forty-six. I had already ascertained that fact this morning purely as a matter of interest.'

'Does the handwriting on the notes give any clue — or the stationery?'

The Doctor held up the notes to the light. 'Hm . . . written in block letters, in good quality ink, on ship's stationery — '

'That might mean it's one of the crew who's written the notes.'

'Since ship's stationery is placed on the desks in every lounge for the passengers' use, your deduction is signally futile.' He peered at the notes again. 'They are written with a fountain pen which has a crossed nib.'

'Well, that's a useful clue,' Miss Frayle asserted, straightening her spectacles. 'All we've got to do is to find the person who has a fountain pen with a crossed nib.'

'Very well, Miss Frayle. Kindly seek out Captain Kenrick, convey my compliments and request him to assemble all the passengers preparatory to our searching them.'

'But that's impossible, Doctor.'

'Precisely!' he snapped. 'Now will you kindly refrain from hindering by your attempts to be *helpful*?' He began to walk down the deck, with his long raking strides, smoking an inevitable Le Sphinx. 'Follow me, Miss Frayle.'

'What are you going to do now?' she demanded, running after him.

'Peruse a book.'

'Read a book?' she echoed, her forehead creased in puzzlement. 'But — what for? Doctor, where are you going?'

'To where one might expect to find reading matter,' he replied briskly, 'the ship's library.'

'I wonder if this ties up with the murder somehow,' she speculated morbidly. 'I wonder where the murderer is now — whether he's planning to strike again.' She broke off with a shudder. 'I was having nightmares about it all last night. Doctor, you must do something!'

He appeared not to be listening to her.

His saturnine features set impassively, he strode into the ship's library, and walked directly to a shelf marked *Reference Books*. He ran a digit finger along the volumes, and paused at a thick book in a scarlet binding.

'Doctor, what on earth do you think you'll find in *Who's Who?*' she asked quickly.

'Merely the information I am seeking, my dear Miss Frayle,' he replied blandly. He placed the heavy volume on a table and flipped the pages. 'Ah, yes, here we are . . . 'Sir Aubrey Halliday . . . born 1897 . . . ' He dwindled off into vague mutterings, but Miss Frayle could hear the essential facts that he was absorbing. 'Son of . . . Educated . . . Called to the Bar in . . . Travelled extensively, particularly France . . . Owner of a number of vineyards and connoisseur of wines. Has contributed numerous articles and written several volumes on this subject . . . Married Mary Daphne St. Clare in 1934 . . . '

He ceased reading and closed the heavy volume with a snap, then handed it to

Miss Frayle for her to replace it on its shelf.

He drummed his knuckles on the table and then rose abruptly saying:

'I think closer acquaintance with the gentleman might furnish me with even more information.'

'You mean you're going to see Sir Aubrey?'

He nodded. 'Yes, I see no reason why I should not pay him a call. He may have some explanation concerning these two mysterious communications.'

She followed him to the door eagerly.

'May I come with you?' she asked.

He looked down at her with studied frankness.

'I feel on this occasion your presence might be somewhat superfluous,' he retorted.

She refused to be shaken off, and steadily she trotted after him.

'But supposing there's any danger? You'll need me,' she declared.

That sardonic light crept into his narrowed eyes again.

'Ah! That's a contingency I had

overlooked. However since you yourself described Sir Aubrey as being 'a harmless and charming' man, I cannot appreciate the plausibility of your concern for my safety.'

'I may have been mistaken,' she protested. 'After all Doctor you're always telling me not to accept the obvious. Sir Aubrey might be a wolf in sheep's clothing — '

He nodded wearily. 'Perhaps, after all, Miss Frayle, you had better remain somewhere within earshot.'

'You mean not to come in with you?' she murmured with plaintive disappointment. 'Just wait about outside the cabin?'

'Precisely, Miss Frayle, and please refrain from appearing suspicious.'

'Of course.'

He lengthened his strides.

'Let us proceed then, forthwith. Cabin number forty-six is it not?'

'That's it, Doctor,' she said more cheerfully now.

Outside cabin forty-six she touched his arm warningly and whispered dramatically:

'Be careful, Doctor! I'll be waiting for you to call me. Signal me if you can't call. I'll understand — I've been in the Girl Guides.'

'Thank you, Miss Frayle,' he replied in a burlesque whisper. His tone indicated that he had no confidence that she was likely to be of any assistance. He tapped on the door.

A cheerful voice shouted: 'Bring them right in.'

Doctor Morelle entered. Sir Aubrey, standing in the middle of the cabin, regarded him with questioning surprise.

'I thought it was the steward with some wineglasses.' Sir Aubrey began. 'Your features seem familiar, sir. Do I — ?'

'I am Doctor Morelle.'

The Doctor closed the door behind him, adding:

'This is a social visit.'

'Splendid! Only too glad to have someone to talk to, Doctor. I'm finding the trip a little lonely. Do sit down.'

The Doctor sank on to the settee, crossed his long legs, and watched the other man through a cloud of cigarette smoke

'You are Sir Aubrey Halliday, are you not?' he asked softly.

'I am. Ah, thank you.' He accepted a Le Sphinx from the Doctor Morelle's thin gold case. 'Perhaps you'll join me in a glass of port? I've just asked a steward to bring me some wineglasses. He should be here any minute.' Sir Aubrey paused, expecting the Doctor to take up the small talk, but Doctor Morelle merely studied his host with impassive thoroughness. 'Hm . . . surprisingly calm voyage we're having,' the other continued absently. 'Captain says we should make New York in five days — '

He broke off as there was a tap on the door. 'Ah, here's the steward,' he said in a relieved tone. 'Come in.'

A steward appeared with wineglasses on a tray.

'On the table, sir?'

'Yes please. Thanks.' Sir Aubrey gave him a coin. 'Hand me that bottle of port from its cradle, will you?'

Sir Aubrey's manner was that of the genial host, as he turned to the Doctor with his bushy eyebrows raised.

'You will join me, won't you?' he hazarded. 'This is some very special wine. Sixty-year-old stuff. Like your opinion on it.'

The Doctor permitted himself a faintly deprecating smile.

'Thank you,' he acknowledged, 'but I'm afraid, however, I'm not the authority you are.'

The steward touched the bottle, and glanced inquiringly at the host.

'Shall I open it, sir?' he asked.

'No, I'll manage. That'll be all.'

'Thank you, sir.' The steward paused in the doorway and added: 'Oh, I just found a young woman hanging about outside — eavesdropper, she looked like — '

'A young woman?' Sir Aubrey echoed, his eyebrows knitting into a frown.

'Yes, sir, seemed rather suspicious to me. She said she was tying her shoelaces . . . but she was wearing shoes without any!'

'Really! This is most extraordinary.'

'Yes sir. She's cleared off, but I thought I'd warn you.'

'Yes, thank you, steward. I'll ring

should I need you again.'

'Very good, sir.'

Sir Aubrey fingered the wineglasses.

'Young woman?' he pondered. 'Wonder who she could be?'

'I cannot imagine.' The Doctor's face was an impassive mask.

The other man shrugged his massive shoulders.

'Ah, well . . . let's open this bottle.' He tugged at the corkscrew, his face tensing with the effort and irritation. 'Darn the cork. It's rotting with age. Ah, here it comes!'

There was a comforting plop, and the cork came raggedly out of the bottle.

'Now, you try this, Doctor,' Sir Aubrey said, pouring the wine into a glass. 'A toast — your good health, sir.'

Doctor Morelle politely rose to his feet. He stood with his back towards the door. He raised his glass in his left hand. With his right hand, unseen by the host, he felt along the door, grasped the key and removed it, holding it securely in his hand.

He smiled thinly. 'I think a toast to

absent friends might also be not out of place.'

'Absent friends?'

'With special good feelings to one particular person — Sir Aubrey Halliday,' the Doctor continued enigmatically. 'By the way have you encountered Sir Aubrey lately?'

'Encountered him?' echoed the other, goggling at the Doctor above his glass. 'What the devil are you talking about, man? *I* am Aubrey Halliday.'

The Doctor flicked the ash off his Le Sphinx.

'On the contrary,' he murmured softly. 'You are a liar and an impostor.'

'What's that? What!' the man blustered, veins showing on his forehead. Shooting out his right hand he grabbed the port bottle and with the full force of his powerful shoulders he sent it hurtling. The Doctor ducked, the bottle broke against the door and the contents spattered over his collar and shirt. Adroitly he opened the door, grasping the key that he had taken and inserted it on the outside turning the lock.

Mopping his shirt and collar he turned a deaf ear to the angry thumping on the other side of the door marked Cabin Forty-six.

Round the corner of the corridor, he encountered Miss Frayle. She took one glance at his red-smeared shirt and collar and flung her arms round him in possessive anxiety.

'Doctor — I deserted you — and you've been injured — mortally!' she babbled.

He smiled ironically.

'Kindly extricate yourself, Miss Frayle,' he commanded. 'You are impeding my progress.'

'But you're hurt, Doctor,' she insisted.

'On the contrary.' He mopped at the liquid on his collar. 'I've merely been baptised in port wine — fortuitously vintage port, which is, I suppose, a consolation.' He smiled thinly and explained: 'After expressing my appreciation of a glassful of my host's wine, he gratuitously presented me with the — er — bottle.'

He began to stride down the corridor.

'Where are you going?'

'To my cabin to change my habiliments,' he replied. 'Meanwhile, my dear Miss Frayle, you would be of some slight assistance if you would proceed to the Master-at-Arms and inform him that I have under lock and key, in cabin forty-six, an impostor and probably a murderer! Hurry, any moment the man might escape and commit another ferocious attack — '

She was already running frenziedly towards the deck. Above the pounding of her pulse she heard the Doctor's sardonic laughter following her mockingly.

* * *

Later, after the Master-at-Arms had taken charge of the man who had called himself Sir Aubrey Halliday, Miss Frayle encountered Doctor Morelle, wearing a change of clothes, stepping on to the sun deck. She ran up to him excitedly.

'The man who impersonated Sir Aubrey has confessed to the Master-at-Arms to throwing Lawrence Devereux overboard,' she informed him excitedly.

'As I anticipated.'

'And to think that murderer had crept into my cabin,' she said with a shudder. 'What do you think he was after?'

'Probably he was searching for incriminating letters of a passionate nature which would give him grounds to blackmail you later.'

'He'd have been unlucky!' she said somewhat ruefully. She looked up at him with frank admiration. 'Oh, Doctor, I'm so relieved you weren't hurt. I'm dying to know how you discovered the man was an impostor. Do tell me.'

Doctor Morelle exhaled a cloud of blue smoke from his cigarette. Negligently he leaned against the deck rail.

'From the *Who's Who* directory I learned that the real Sir Aubrey was an expert on wines,' he said. 'When, therefore, the man in cabin forty-six proceeded to extract the cork from a sixty-year-old bottle of port and pour its contents straight into the glass, it was evident he was an impostor.'

'I don't see why,' she puzzled.

'Anyone with an elementary knowledge

knows old wines of this type have to be decanted before they are served because of the crust which forms on them. This sediment would ruin the wine if poured with it into the glass. It was virtually impossible for one as expert as the real Sir Aubrey Halliday to commit such an unpardonable error.'

Miss Frayle straightened her spectacles.

'I think you took rather a chance, though, Doctor,' she observed. 'The real Sir Aubrey might have been absent-minded at that moment.'

'I cannot, I fear, subscribe to your view, Miss Frayle,' he said gravely. 'In point of fact, the impostor made two other mistakes in connection with a matter on which he was supposed to be expert.'

'Two mistakes? What were they?'

'He asked the waiter to remove the bottle from the cradle, which is especially made to aid in decanting the wine. Secondly, no knowledgeable person would wish to drink a wine of that age within twenty-four hours of it being poured.'

'Oh, I think you're wonderful!'

'The man who called himself Sir

Aubrey Halliday was patently a confidence trickster,' continued the Doctor. 'No doubt he had actually stolen or received the passport and documents belonging to the real Sir Aubrey, and assumed his identity as a cloak of respectability for his nefarious activities. The man he murdered was, no doubt, a blackmailer,' he theorised, 'who recognised the impostor for the crook he was and, threatening to extort money from him — '

'Oh, no, you're wrong there, Doctor,' Miss Frayle put in with bright triumph. 'The impostor told the Master-at-Arms that the murdered man was an accomplice. They had quarrelled over the division of some spoil — '

'An inconsequential detail,' he snapped. 'Not in the least affecting the scientific elucidation of our mystery.' He rounded on her with quick irritation. 'At least I did not make the error of saying I was tying up my shoelaces when my shoes were of the plain variety. In spite of the fact that I was never a member of the Girl Guides!'

She coughed embarrassedly, and blushed. 'I really did my best not to look suspicious,' she murmured, and quickly she decided to change the subject. 'But who was it who sent those mysterious notes?'

'Obviously Mrs. Van der Husen,' he said, dismissing that point. 'She would doubtless have some recollection of the real Sir Aubrey — no doubt she had encountered him briefly during her travels, and after perusing the ship's list, and in her snobbish manner — ' he broke off as he noticed Miss Frayle gesticulating wildly.

Mrs. Van der Husen had sidled along the deck rail, and was standing directly behind the Doctor, listening to every word he uttered.

'Kindly control those convulsive movements, Miss Frayle,' he continued. 'As I was saying, Mrs. Van der Husen, with her overdeveloped and thoroughly nauseating snobbish instincts, would know the real Sir Aubrey only by sight. No doubt if she were here now she would claim life-long acquaintance with that gentleman, as she did when she encountered me. However, she had not the moral courage, being a feckless and scatter-brained female, to expose the impostor openly. She resorted to the cowardly device of anonymous notes.'

Mrs. Van der Husen, a grim smile on her carmined lips, moved from behind the Doctor and stood facing him.

'You have made another error, Doctor Morelle!' she said icily. 'I know the real Sir Aubrey *intimately*. In fact, when I met you at the American Embassy in Paris, my *dear* Doctor Morelle, six years ago, I was then *married* to the *real* Sir Aubrey Halliday.' She pulled her mink coat round her with great dignity. 'Good afternoon!'

5

The case of the Secret Heart

The telephone rang on Doctor Morelle's desk, He glanced up irritably from his note-making, and glanced across at Miss Frayle, where she sat at her own desk, catching up on some filing.

'I'm busy,' he snapped.

Miss Frayle sighed, and got up. She came around to her employer's desk and placed her hand on the ivory telephone. 'You're out — unless it's a matter of life and death?'

The Doctor merely grunted at her rhetorical question and continued writing. Miss Frayle picked up the receiver.

'Hello? This is Doctor Morelle's house.'

'Roses — these roses — ' The man's voice at the other end of the phone was strangulated, as if he was choking.

Miss Frayle furrowed her brows, 'What — ?'

The choking voice resumed, 'There's a bowl of roses on the breakfast table and the scent — I can't get my breath.'

'Who is that?' queried Miss Frayle, sharply.

'It's Mr. Redford. David Redford,' the caller gasped for breath. 'Tell Dr. Morelle — '

Miss Frayle placed her hand over the receiver, and blinked at Dr. Morelle. 'Doctor Morelle — '

The Doctor had noticed her movement and laid aside his pen with a sigh. 'What is it, Miss Frayle?'

'It's Mr. Redford. He sounds very ill,'

'I'll speak to him.' The Doctor reached out his hand for the phone, then spoke into it. 'Doctor Morelle here.'

Miss Frayle went back to her desk.

'I'm choking to death, Doctor,' the gasping voice resumed. 'This asthma. Someone put roses on the table — '

'Take the adrenalin injection I prescribed for you,' Dr. Morelle said briefly.

'I have — but it doesn't help. I've got to see you!' There was real desperation in Redford's voice.

158

'Very well,' Dr. Morelle conceded.
'I'll come right away.'

As Dr. Morelle replaced the receiver, Miss Frayle spoke sympathetically. 'Poor Mr. Redford, it must be dreadful for him. What causes this asthma, Doctor?'

'Asthma is a spasmodic condition of the tubes or bronchi that lead to the lungs. The patient is unable to exhale the dead air, and feels that he is suffocating.'

Miss Frayle was reflecting on the call. 'How can roses give him asthma? They're such lovely flowers.'

'The symbol of love, eh, Miss Frayle?' Doctor Morelle smiled sardonically.

'I wasn't thinking of them in that way, Doctor.'

'Never mind, so long as you think of them.'

'What do you mean?' Miss Frayle asked, puzzled.

'He has been an unresponsive patient, now the moment has arrived to accelerate the treatment. Hurry out at once and buy some roses.'

'Roses, Doctor Morelle?' Miss Frayle

became flustered. 'For me — ?'

'Get them from Finlayson's in Oxford Street.'

'*Finlayson's?* But, Doctor — ?'

Doctor Morelle nodded firmly. 'Three dozen roses,' he elaborated. 'Red roses, which symbolize love and romance to you, but which to Mr. Redford symbolize suffocation.'

'You want me to get them right away?'

'Yes, before Mr. Redford arrives.'

'Yes, Doctor Morelle.' Miss Frayle sighed and got to her feet.

* * *

Miss Frayle responded to the sound of the ringing doorbell. She went out into the hall and opened the door of Doctor Morelle's Harley Street residence.

As she had anticipated, it was David Redford. He was a dark-haired, thin-faced man in his early thirties. He spoke chokingly:

'Is Doctor Morelle — ?'

'He's waiting for you, Mr. Redford,' Miss Frayle assured him, and stepped back, holding the door handle with one hand, and inviting him in with the other.

She closed the door, then turned to give him a sympathetic smile. 'I do hope you're feeling better.'

'Yes, thanks. But I really thought I'd had it that time.'

'I'm so sorry. Come this way.' Miss Frayle led the way across the hall to Doctor Morelle's office.

'I felt as if I'd never get my breath,' Redford said miserably, as he followed her. She opened a door and went inside the room, Redford following close behind her.

'Mr. Redford, Doctor Morelle.'

Doctor Morelle got up from his desk and came forward.

'Come in. All right, Miss Frayle. Please wait in the other room.'

Miss Frayle nodded disappointedly and closed the door behind her.

Doctor Morelle pointed to a chair near to his desk as he walked towards it. 'Sit down, won't you?' he invited.

Redford did so somewhat reluctantly. He was staring at something on Doctor

Morelle's desk with considerable trepidation.

'Those roses — ' he choked.

'What — ?' Doctor Morelle spoke blandly as he resumed his own seat.

'Those roses on your desk — '

Doctor Morelle glanced casually at the large bowl at the side of his desk. 'Miss Frayle must have put them there.' He affected slight surprise, then added reprovingly: 'How careless of her.'

Redford began to shake, one hand to his throat. 'I can't breathe — the perfume — I'm choking. Give me a shot, Doctor. Adrenalin — '

Doctor Morelle smiled faintly. 'Relax, Mr. Redford, relax.'

'I'll choke to death,' Redford gasped.

'I'll give you an injection.' Dr. Morelle got up and moved to a glass-fronted medical cabinet.

Redford had stood up. 'This asthma — '

'Let me help you off with your coat,' Doctor Morelle murmured.

'Thanks.'

'Now undo your cuff-link. Your sleeve a bit higher — '

'Hurry, Doctor,' Redford choked.

Doctor Morelle gave the injection. 'That's it, now try and relax.'

'Phew, that's better.' Redford sank down into his chair. He was rapidly calming. 'I really thought I was going to die.'

'Death, a necessary end, will come when it comes,' Doctor Morelle pronounced. He returned the hypodermic to the cabinet and resumed his seat behind his desk.

Redford looked at him quizzically. 'How were those roses left there, when you were expecting me?'

Doctor Morelle regarded the bowl. 'I must reprimand Miss Frayle for her carelessness. According to her they symbolize romance.' He stretched out a hand. 'Look at this one.'

Redford averted his eyes as Doctor Morelle held out a rose from the bowl. 'No, really, I — ' He broke off with astonishment. 'Why, why, it's made of paper — '

'Precisely.' Dr. Morelle smiled sardonically. 'A paper rose. They're all paper roses.'

'But I don't understand — ?' Redford looked his bafflement. 'You mean — ?'

'Miss Frayle has just brought them back from the shop in Oxford Street. Very realistic don't you think?'

Redford shook his head. 'Paper roses — not real roses at all.'

'No more than the adrenalin in the hypodermic injection,' Doctor Morelle admitted. 'It was merely sterilised distilled water.'

'Water?' Redford said weakly.

'Paper roses and water.'

'But what are you getting at?' Redford stood up. 'What does this mean?'

'It means,' Doctor Morelle said deliberately, 'that your asthma attacks are not the result of an allergy to roses, they are caused by a neurosis, A fear of something you are afraid to reveal.'

'A fear — ?' Redford sat down again.

Doctor Morelle leaned forward and fixed his patient with a penetrating gaze. 'Therefore the next stop, Mr. Redford, is to discover what it is you are frightened of.'

Redford struggled with his thoughts for

a moment, then squared his shoulders and seemed to come to a decision.

'You're right, Doctor Morelle. It was seven or eight weeks ago. I'd gone up to Uncle Herbert's bedroom. He wasn't there, the bathroom door was open and quite by chance I glanced in, and there he was in the bath. He'd slipped and hit his head. I started to pull him out, and then this extraordinary sensation came over me — '

Doctor Morelle nodded gravely. 'An overwhelming compulsion to leave him as he was?'

'Everything flashed through my mind, the fact that his will was in my favour and that by leaving him I wouldn't really be guilty of having murdered him.'

'But in fact you got your uncle out of his bath?'

'Yes.' Redford expelled a long breath as he recalled the traumatic event. 'I carried him into the bedroom and within a few minutes he'd recovered and was perfectly all right. I left a couple of hours later and got a taxi home. It was dark, and I hadn't been in the taxi long when I noticed the scent of roses. And then the roses became absolutely overpowering, and I had to stop the taxi. In the corner was a bunch of roses. They'd been left there by a previous passenger. By now I was almost choking to death, and I had to get another taxi to take me home.'

'At last we are arriving at the truth,' Doctor Morelle murmured.

Redford looked a little shame-faced. 'I know, I've not been very frank with you.'

'This was the first asthmatic attack which you attributed to roses?' Doctor Morelle asked sharply.

Redford nodded. 'That first attack passed off, but that night I couldn't sleep. I kept on realising how near death my uncle had been, and it would have been my fault.'

'Your uncle's will plays an important part in this matter,' Doctor Morelle commented.

Redford shrugged. 'It's because he keeps changing it. Sometimes he gets the idea that he'll leave the lot to me, another time he changes his mind and leaves it all to his sister, Aunt Henrietta. Then he'll get another idea and leave half to us each; or he'll decide he ought to leave some to Darrell, the manservant who's been with him about twelve years, It's almost a joke, except there's nothing very funny about being left twenty thousand pounds.'

'And even less amusing not to be left it,' Doctor Morelle murmured dryly.

Redford sighed. 'He drives old Coghill, his lawyer, up the wall.'

'What is your aunt's reaction to all this?' Doctor Morelle asked thoughtfully.

'That's pretty eccentric, too,' Redford smiled faintly. 'I tell you that old house is like something you've never seen. Aunt Henrietta, obsessed with her aviary of tropical birds, and Uncle who spends hours totting up how much money he has and deciding who's to get it when he dies.'

'No one else occupies the house?'

'Only Darrell, the manservant I mentioned. How he copes, I don't know. Except that there's the chance he'll collect several thousand. In fact, he might get the lot.'

Doctor Morelle reflected for a moment,

then asked: 'And you are a frequent visitor to the house?'

'Yes, I'm always in and out. My flat's only the other side of Wimbledon common. They're lonely, no one else ever goes to see them.'

'Your motive for giving this eccentric old couple the pleasure of your company would be purely disinterested?'

Redford hesitated. 'Er — yes, of course.'

'Come now, Mr. Redford,' Doctor Morelle spoke sharply. 'You have made it clear that you might inherit a large sum of money upon your uncle's death. Obviously you are profoundly inhibited by the prospect.'

Redford looked uncomfortable. 'I might as well confess it, Doctor Morelle.'

'Confession is good for the soul, Mr. Redford.'

'Trouble is, I'm flat broke,' Redford admitted frankly. 'I've tried to hold down half-a-dozen jobs in the past couple of years without success.'

'So that your visits to the house at Wimbledon are quite calculated.'

'I suppose you might say so,' Redford agreed.

'There is precious little supposition about it,' Doctor Morelle snapped. 'You are doing your utmost to remain in your uncle's affections in the hope that you will benefit from his death.'

'In my secret heart, yes,' Redford admitted quietly.

'It is into your secret heart that we are seeing,' Doctor Morelle said relentlessly. 'There lies your subconscious guilt-complexes and your obsessive fancy that roses give you asthma.'

'What can I do to help myself?'

'My advice,' Doctor Morelle told him, 'is to concentrate your mind more upon trying to obtain some employment which will make you independent of any legacy,'

'All right,' Redford promised, 'I'll pull myself together and see if I can't land a job and stick to it.'

There came a gentle knocking on the door, which then opened. Miss Frayle came into the room.

'Oh, Doctor Morelle — ' she began.

'Mr. Redford is just going, Miss Frayle,' he told her. 'He'll be ringing up for an appointment in a week's time.'

Redford scrambled to his feet. 'Thanks very much, Doctor, for all you've done. I'll try and sort myself out.'

Miss Frayle glanced out of the window at the briskly departing figure of Redford before settling at her desk.

'Mr. Redford seems very much better now, Doctor Morelle, than when he arrived.'

'I'm glad you think so, Miss Frayle.'

Miss Frayle glanced at the paper roses. 'Fancy having those horrid asthma attacks for no reason at all.'

'There *was* a reason,' Doctor Morelle corrected, 'and if he will concentrate his powers fully upon the task of reintegrating himself a cure will be effected.'

'Oh well,' Miss Frayle said blithely, 'where there's a will there's a way.'

Doctor Morelle gave a dry chuckle. 'There are moments, Miss Frayle, when your banal utterances strike nearer the truth than you know.'

Miss Frayle frowned. 'I still don't

understand why I had to rush out and buy those silly paper roses.'

★ ★ ★

In a house near Wimbledon Common, Henrietta Vickers was talking softly to the birds in her aviary.

'Sweet, sweet, there you are. We must cover you up for the night.'

'Are you there, Henrietta?' the voice of her brother sounded faintly above the twittering from somewhere outside the aviary.

'Yes, what is it you want?' she responded.

'Henrietta, where are you?' Vickers called, more loudly.

'I'm here, Herbert, what do you want?'

Vickers opened the door to the aviary. 'Henrietta — oh, there you are.'

'What d'you *want*?' Henrietta repeated, with a touch of exasperation.

Vickers cocked a hand to his ear. 'Eh? Can't hear a thing with these blasted birds.'

Henrietta sighed resignedly. 'Is it

anything important?'

'Of course it's important,' Vickers snapped. 'Otherwise I wouldn't want to talk to you about it.'

Henrietta picked up a birdcage cover. 'I'll be with you in a minute.'

'All right, I won't talk here, with all this noise, I'm going to the sitting room.'

'I'll come in a minute . . . ' Henrietta turned to gaze fondly at her feathered friends. 'Sweet, sweet, it's time to go to sleep my pets.'

Returning to the sitting room, Vickers eased himself gingerly into his favourite chair. He began to gently hum and whistle to himself as he waited for his sister.

'Now, what is it you want to talk to me about, Herbert?' Henrietta asked, coming into the room.

'Yes, now then. It's about David.'

'David, what about him? Do hurry up, I've got to talk to Darrell about dinner. All I want is a little consommé, but you'll want an omelette.'

'Do you realise he's only been to see us once in the last week?' Vickers frowned.

'Not like him at all, he used to be here almost every day.'

Henrietta shrugged. 'Personally, I'm very glad.'

Vickers looked his surprise. 'But I thought you liked him?'

'Of course I like David, isn't he my nephew?'

'He's my nephew, too,' Vickers said heavily. 'Why doesn't he come and see us as much as he used to?'

'For the reason he's given us, I hope. He's trying to get himself a job.'

'You really believe that?' Vickers asked sharply. 'He's had other jobs and none of them have been any good.'

'And do you want to know why, Herbert?' Henrietta looked at her elderly brother shrewdly. 'Because he was thinking of the money he'll get from you.'

Vickers shook his head. 'What an absolute exaggeration.'

'You know you enjoy having this power over him, of being able to leave him money or not as you wish.'

'I don't know what your chattering is about,' Vickers protested.

'You may be an eccentric old man — '

'You're a fine one to talk!' Vickers snorted. 'Those blasted tropical birds!'

Henrietta shrugged. 'I don't deny it. But I haven't got twenty thousand pounds to leave when I die.'

'You will have, if I die first and leave the lot to you.'

Henrietta smiled faintly. 'I don't care whether I get your money or not, and you know it. It doesn't give me any sleepless nights, but this was why David couldn't hang onto his jobs and I hope he's realised at last that it's bad for him to rely on you.'

'But why shouldn't I change my will as often as I like?' Vickers spread his hands. 'If it amuses me to do so?'

'No reason at all. It's your money.'

'In any case that wasn't what I wanted to talk to you about. It was not David not coming to see us so much — ' Vickers broke off as Henrietta began to get to her feet, 'What is it?'

'I thought I heard someone outside the door . . . ' Henrietta moved quickly to the door and yanked it open.

Standing right outside, looking somewhat off balance, was Darrell, their manservant.

'What is it, Darrell?' Henrietta demanded sharply.

'Nothing, Miss.' Darrell straightened himself.

'What were you doing? Tying up your shoelaces?'

'I wanted to ask you about dinner tonight,' Darrell said smoothly.

'All right, I'll come and talk to you.' Henrietta looked back to where her brother still sat in his armchair. 'An omelette for you, Herbert?'

'Yes, Henrietta.'

As the door closed, Vickers stretched and smiled to himself. 'All this talk about Wills and dying! Why, I feel good enough for another twenty years.'

* * *

It was late evening in the Vickers household. The Grandfather Clock in the hall was striking nine.

In the sitting room, Henrietta laid aside

the book she had been reading. 'I don't know about you, Herbert, but I'm going to bed.'

Her brother looked up from reading the evening newspaper. He took a puff from his cigar, and returned it carefully to the ashtray resting on the wide, flat arm of his chair. 'What is the time?'

'It's just struck nine.' Henrietta smothered a yawn. 'It's been a long day for me; I was up early this morning . . . ' she broke off and glanced towards the door as Darrell knocked lightly, and came in.

'Will you require anything further tonight?' he asked respectfully.

'No thank you, Darrell,' Vickers said, glancing at his sister for confirmation.

'You can lock up,' Henrietta added.

'Very good, Miss.' Darrell turned to go.

'Oh, Darrell — ' Vickers said suddenly, and the manservant paused and looked back. An odd expression flickered briefly over his face as he waited for the next.

'Yes, sir?'

'Before you go into town tomorrow morning, come along to the study, will you?' Vickers smiled smugly. 'I'll want you to witness a document for me.'

'Very well, sir.'

'And if you'd ask Mrs. — what's her name? Our new daily help — '

'Mrs. Anderson — ' Henrietta supplied.

Vickers nodded complacently. 'Yes, I'll want her too, as the other witness.'

'Very good, sir.'

Vickers was watching the manservant closely, and enjoying the moment. Had he detected a slight tightening of his lips? 'Mr. Coghill will be there.'

'Then you'll want coffee, sir?'

'Yes, he must have his cup of coffee.' Vickers smiled faintly. 'You've quite got to know his habits.'

'Well, Mr. Coghill's been coming here often enough,' Darrell said, dryly.

Vickers gave a little chuckle. 'That's what my sister's complaining of. Eh, Henrietta?' As his sister remained silent, he looked back to the manservant. 'Doesn't like lawyers. Good night, Darrell.'

'Good night, sir. Good night, Miss.'

'Good night, Darrell,' Henrietta said.

She waited until he had closed the door, then looked at her brother with mild annoyance. 'So you're going to change your blessed will again.'

'I might, I might,' Vickers answered complacently, puffing at his cigar.

Henrietta got to her feet. 'I'll just go and see that my birds are safe, then I'm off to bed.'

'Good night, my dear.'

Henrietta paused at the door and looked back.

'Don't fall asleep and set fire to yourself with that cigar.'

'I'll be going up to bed myself in a few minutes.'

After his sister had left, Vickers sat for a few minutes as he finished his cigar. He carefully stubbed it out, then folded his newspaper and laid it on the other arm of the chair.

Humming and whistling softly to himself, he went up the stairs. Half way up he paused and smiled. 'I think I'll run a bath before I go to bed.'

Reaching his personal bathroom, Vickers turned on the hot and cold taps. As they ran into the bath, he went into his bedroom through an adjoining door, and began to undress.

'Wonder what suit I should wear tomorrow?' he mused to himself, 'Must look smart for old Coghill. My tweed jacket — or the black suit? Or will that look as if I'm in mourning?' He chuckled. 'Perhaps not quite the thing for discussing my will. No, I think I'll put on the brown suit . . . '

He donned his dressing gown, and moved back into the bathroom. He took out a new bar of soap from the pocket of his dressing gown, unwrapped it, placed it in the plastic wire tray hanging over the hot tap.

Bending down, he dipped his hand into the bath water. 'Water's hot enough, just right,' he murmured. He let the taps run for another few moments, then turned them off.

He was just about to take off his dressing gown, when the telephone extension in his bedroom began ringing.

Vickers frowned in annoyance. 'Dear me, who could that be ringing? Suppose

I'd better answer it.' Bare-footed, he went back into his bedroom, and picked up the receiver.

'Hello? Oh, hello. No, I can't now, I've just ran my bath. Ring again in half an hour. All right, goodbye.'

A few moments later, Vickers was luxuriating in his warm bath, humming and whistling to himself.

The bathroom door began to open.

'Who's there? Who — ?'

The door creaked wide open.

'You — ?' Vickers gasped. 'What the devil are you doing here?' Fear edged his voice as he tried, ineffectively, to stand up. The water splashed as he fell back.

'Get out — Get out, I tell you — *Let me go — Let go — !*'

⋆   ⋆   ⋆

Miss Frayle answered the telephone.

'Doctor Morelle's house,' she said complacently, then tensed as she heard the agitated voice at the other end of the line.

'This is Mr. Redford, Miss Frayle — '

'Oh, it's you, Mr. Redford?'

'Can I speak to Doctor Morelle, please? It's very urgent!'

'All right, Mr. Redford. He's in the laboratory, will you hold on?'

Miss Frayle hurried out of Doctor Morelle's office, and entered his laboratory without knocking.

'Doctor Morelle — ' she began.

'Ah, Miss Frayle, I wanted to ask you about these slides which had been under this microscope, and . . . ' He broke off as he became aware of Miss Frayle's agitated manner.

'It's Mr. Redford,' she said excitedly. 'He's on the telephone.'

'Redford?' Doctor Morelle raised his eyebrows. 'At this time of night?'

'He says it's very urgent!'

Doctor Morelle laid aside the apparatus he had been working on. 'I'll speak to him. Did he sound as if troubled again by asthma?'

Miss Frayle reflected. 'No, but he was very agitated.'

A minute later Doctor Morelle was back at his desk, picking up the phone.

'Doctor Morelle here,' he said crisply.

'This is David Redford — It's my uncle — he's just been found dead — in his bath!'

'Where are you speaking from, Mr. Redford?'

'My uncle's house at Wimbledon. Can you come over as soon as possible?'

'Did you discover your uncle?'

'No, it was my aunt.'

'Where were you at the time?' Doctor Morelle asked sharply.

'I — I — that's just it. You see, it was just as I called at the house on my way to my flat that it happened. But I didn't do it, Doctor Morelle, I didn't do it.'

'I will come at once.' Doctor Morelle replaced the receiver and looked at Miss Frayle. 'Is it a very pleasant night for a drive, Miss Frayle?'

His secretary looked at him in surprise. 'Not specially, there's a bit of a wind, and the forecast said rain.'

'What a pity.'

'Why?'

'Because we are driving to Wimbledon immediately.'

Miss Frayle, seated alongside Doctor Morelle as he drove through the night to Wimbledon, peered through the windscreen.

'Those look like the gates, Doctor, just ahead.'

'Then we will turn in there.' Doctor Morelle expertly spun the wheel.

'Yes, I can just read the name of the house in the headlights,' Miss Frayle said. 'It looks a tumbledown place, from what one can see of it in the dark.'

Doctor Morelle brought the car to a halt, and a few moments later a light appeared at the front door of the house. The door opened and a figure was silhouetted in the entrance.

'There's someone at the door,' Miss Frayle said unnecessarily, as she and the Doctor got out of the car.

'Doubtless, Mr. Redford will be waiting for us,' Doctor Morelle said, as he locked the car. Turning, he added: 'Come along. Miss Frayle.'

Miss Frayle clutched at the top buttons

of her overcoat, and glanced apprehensively skywards. 'It's blowing up for a storm, all right. Look at the clouds across the moon.'

Redford was waiting for them as they came up to the front door.

'Thank goodness you've come, Doctor Morelle. Hello, Miss Frayle.'

'I'm sorry to hear your news,' Miss Frayle said sympathetically, as she and the Doctor came inside. She saw that Redford looked under a considerable strain.

Redford closed the door quickly. 'Come upstairs to Uncle's bedroom. I'll lead the way.'

'Where is your Aunt?' Doctor Morelle asked, as they mounted the stairs.

Redford glanced back over his shoulder. 'In her own room, the shock proved a bit much for her.'

'Poor thing,' Miss Frayle murmured.

Redford paused on the landing, and looked at Miss Frayle and the Doctor as they reached the top of the stairs, 'When she found Uncle in the bath, she called Darrell and they got him out of the bath.

Darrell tried artificial respiration, but it was no good. However, you'd better see him for yourself.' He pointed to the nearest door behind him. 'In here, Doctor, we got him onto the bed.'

Inside the bedroom, Doctor Morelle crossed quickly to the unmoving figure of Herbert Vickers on the bed. He lifted aside the thin sheet that covered him, and bent to make a swift examination. In the background, Miss Frayle was averting her eyes.

'I fear your Uncle is dead, Mr. Redford,' he pronounced, straightening.

Redford sighed. 'We did our best to revive him.'

'What was the time approximately, when your aunt discovered him?' Doctor Morelle questioned.

'Just before I phoned you.'

'That was about a quarter to eleven,' Miss Frayle put in.

Redford nodded unhappily. 'Yes. He had his bath just after nine. The water was cold.'

'Has the bath been emptied?' Doctor Morelle asked.

'No.'

'Then I'd like to test the water.'

'By all means.' Redford moved to open the connecting door to the bathroom.

Doctor Morelle glanced at his secretary as she made to follow them. 'Wait here, Miss Frayle.'

'Yes, Doctor,' Miss Frayle said uneasily, still averting her eyes from the tragic figure on the bed.

Entering the bathroom, Doctor Morelle observed that the windows were closed, and there was a certain amount of condensation. He bent to trail his hand in the bath water.

'As you say, it is cold. How is the water heated?'

Redford indicated a cupboard. 'By an immersion heater — the tank's inside here. There's another bathroom at the other end of the passage, adjoining Aunt's room.'

'I see.' Doctor Morelle frowned thoughtfully.

Redford looked at him anxiously. 'Doctor Morelle — the reason I sent for you is that — don't you see — ?'

'No need to explain the obvious.' Doctor Morelle shrugged. 'You fear you will be suspected of being concerned with your uncle's death?'

'If he's altered his will in my favour — as he may have done — it'll look black against me, won't it?' Redford said miserably.

'You're taking a somewhat hysterical viewpoint,' Doctor Morelle spoke dismissively. 'Plenty of evidence will be forthcoming to show whether or not death was the result of natural causes. Let us return to the other room.'

Rejoining Miss Frayle in the bedroom, Doctor Morelle moved over to the bed, and stared thoughtfully at the corpse, then glanced at Redford, standing nearby disconsolately.

'The *assumption* is that your uncle suffered a heart attack while having his bath?'

'Or that he just fainted,' Redford suggested.

'That would appear to be unlikely,' Doctor Morelle snapped.

'Why, Doctor?' Miss Frayle's averted

gaze shifted to look at him. 'What do you mean?'

'Had he fainted he would presumably have fallen back against the bath. Water entering his mouth or nose as a result would bring him out of his fainting attack.'

'You mean he must have slipped like he did that other time I told you about?' Redford said hopefully. 'And struck his head?'

Doctor Morelle shook his head. 'In this case there is no evidence of bruising.'

Redford frowned. 'Then it must have been his heart.'

'Had he ever been affected by such a heart attack before?' Doctor Morelle asked sharply.

'No, I don't think he has.'

'I can see no external indication that he suffered from any heart condition,' Doctor Morelle said, turning.

'Doctor Morelle, what are you saying — ' Miss Frayle's eyes widened.

'I am saying nothing, beyond that there seems to be no evidence so far to suggest the cause of death. The post mortem may reveal something significant.' Doctor Morelle regarded Redford keenly. 'Perhaps I could see your aunt?'

'Yes, I'll take you to her.'

Doctor Morelle glanced at his secretary as she stood uncertainly. 'Miss Frayle, would you telephone about a doctor?'

'Yes, Doctor.'

'I'll give you the phone number of uncle's doctor,' Redford offered.

'Thank you.' Miss Frayle looked uneasily at the telephone beside the dead man's bed. Redford quickly realised her discomfiture at the proximity of the corpse.

'You can telephone from the sitting room downstairs,' he suggested. He turned to the Doctor as a thought struck him. 'What about the police?'

'We may leave that for the moment,' Doctor Morelle replied suavely.

'All right.' Redford opened the door. 'Aunt Henrietta's room is along the passage.'

Miss Frayle followed them out thankfully, and made her way downstairs to telephone.

A few moments later the two men were

in the old woman's bedroom. She was sat up in bed, wearing a dressing gown and a night cap. Redford made the introductions, and Doctor Morelle began to question her on the tragic events of the evening.

'I said goodnight to Herbert an hour and a half before, Doctor Morelle, and had gone to bed,' Henrietta recalled.

'But you got up and went to see him again for some reason?'

Henrietta nodded. 'It was this ridiculous business of his constantly changing his will.'

Doctor Morelle glanced at Redford. 'I know something of this idiosyncrasy from your nephew.'

'I'd told him before dinner how upsetting it was to people who might be left money. Sometimes one was going to benefit, and then for no reason at all he'd alter his will and cut one clean out.' The old woman sighed heavily. 'The whole thing was quite ludicrous.'

'Do you know if the present will affects you, for instance?' Doctor Morelle asked sharply.

'Frankly no, and I'd got tired of caring. But David had become profoundly affected by prospects of being left all this money. Then after dinner Herbert made it clear he was going to change his will again. He told Darrell, his manservant, that his lawyer would be coming over in the morning and that he'd want Darrell and the daily help as witnesses.'

'The manservant was a beneficiary under the last Will?' Doctor Morelle asked shrewdly.

Henrietta nodded. 'Herbert had told him that he had left him five thousand pounds. And my brother had also said to me that David was to get the rest — plus this house when I die.'

'I see,' Doctor Morelle mused. 'And earlier tonight?'

'I was worried about him changing his will again. I'd asked him to stop all this nonsense, because it was upsetting David. So I went along to his room. He wasn't in his bedroom, but the bathroom door was open and I went in and found him. I shouted for Darrell and together we got him out of the bath.'

'It so happened that about this time your nephew called?' Doctor Morelle questioned, glancing round at Redford, who was standing unhappily behind him.

'He was on his way home, and he stopped to come in and see us,' Henrietta said. 'It was a terrible shock for him. Almost as if he felt that that he himself was in some way responsible for what had happened.'

In the sitting room, Miss Frayle was just replacing the telephone receiver when Doctor Morelle came into the room.

'Oh, there you are, Doctor Morelle,' she said, turning. She pointed to a bowl of roses on a small table near the door. 'I was just thinking how strong the perfume was from that bowl of roses.'

'Their scent is a trifle overpowering,' Doctor Morelle conceded.

'Doctor Morelle — Darrell is coming along now to see you,' Redford said, coming into the room to join them.

'Good. I require a few words with him,' Doctor Morelle said, seating himself in an armchair. Miss Frayle found a seat at the table, looking at the Doctor with a suppressed excitement. She sensed that he might be about to elucidate the mystery of Vickers' death.

Redford looked at Doctor Morelle. 'I'll go back to see Aunt Henrietta, unless you want me to stay here?'

'No.'

'I thought I might ask her to help me to get some tea or coffee,' Redford explained. 'It would occupy her mind.'

'An excellent suggestion,' Doctor Morelle agreed.

Redford glanced behind at the open doorway. 'Here's Darrell. I'll be back in a few minutes.'

'You wish to speak to me, Doctor Morelle?' Darrell said, coming into the room.

Doctor Morelle nodded, and indicated a seat near the table. 'There are one or two matters you might be able to clear up.'

'If I can, Doctor, I will, of course.' Darrell sat down, and moved his chair round slightly so that he directly faced the Doctor.

Miss Frayle stood up, and moved

across to where Doctor Morelle was sitting. She bent down and whispered: 'Doctor. What's that bowl of roses got to do with it?'

'With what, Miss Frayle?' he asked languidly.

'Nothing,' Miss Frayle straightened, still whispering, 'it was just an idea I had.' She returned to her seat as Doctor Morelle ignored her, and fixed his gaze on Darrell.

'Darrell, you assisted Miss Vickers to get her brother out of the bath?'

'That's right. I heard her calling out for help, and I hurried along to the bathroom.'

'Where were you at the time?'

'I was in my own room, getting ready to go to bed.'

Doctor Morelle switched his line of questioning. 'How long have you been in Mr. Vickers' employment?'

Darrell reflected briefly, 'Getting on for twelve years.'

'Would you say that he thought well of you?'

'I like to think so, sir — poor old

gentlemen, I was devoted to him.'

'And he appreciated your devotion, to the extent of making you a beneficiary under his will,' Doctor Morelle said, dryly.

Darrell looked uncomfortable. 'Er — well — '

'That is what I have been given to understand.'

'What I mean is,' Darrell recovered his composure, 'that you didn't know where you stood with him. He'd cut you out of his will as quick as he'd put you in.'

'He must have been a very odd old gentleman,' Miss Frayle remarked.

'He was, Miss.' Darrell glanced at her. 'A proper eccentric — about leaving his money, that is.'

Doctor Morelle leaned forward slightly. 'Had you ever known him suffer from giddiness or heart attacks?'

'I can't say I did Doctor,' Darrell admitted. 'But he was getting on a bit. I suppose the bath was too hot, and he must have fainted.'

'You don't really believe that do you?' Doctor Morelle snapped.

'How do you mean?' Darrell looked uneasy. 'What else could it be?'

'It is hardly conceivable for anyone to drown as a result of a fainting attack while taking a bath,' Doctor Morelle stated deliberately, 'The position in which Miss Vickers found the body lying back against the bath precludes that idea. At the same time there appears to be no external evidence that Vickers suffered from a heart condition.'

Darrell shrugged. 'Perhaps he fell and knocked himself out?'

'I could find no bruises suggestive of that,' Doctor Morelle snapped.

'Then what — ?'

'One other alternative suggests itself . . . Murder!'

Miss Frayle gave a start. 'Murder? But who'd want to murder Mr. Vickers?'

Doctor Morelle turned to her. 'That is a question for the police, Miss Frayle. If you would put a call through to the local police station — '

'Yes, Doctor Morelle.'

He swung his cold gaze back to Darrell, who sat tensed on the edge of his chair.

'Did you, Darrell, observe the marks round the deceased's ankles?'

'His ankles?' Darrell frowned. 'No, I didn't notice anything.'

'Marks on his ankles — ?' Miss Frayle asked, puzzled.

'As if they'd been grasped by someone lifting up the legs, so that he was suddenly submerged.' Doctor Morelle was looking directly at Darrell.

'But who'd want to do a thing like that?' Darrell protested.

'Someone who for instance learned that he was about to alter his will, cutting them out, where they would have benefited,' Doctor Morelle said levelly, his gaze pinning the manservant relentlessly.

'Doctor Morelle, if poor Mr. Vickers was gripped by the ankles, there'll be fingerprints!' Miss Frayle said excitedly.

'Fingerprints — ?' Darrell moistened suddenly dry lips.

Doctor Morelle's eyes took on a sudden gleam. 'That was just what I was about to explain.'

'Fingerprints on wet skin?' Darrell said uneasily.

'And fingerprints never lie,' Doctor Morelle snapped. 'They may be invisible to the naked eye, but there they are. Placed by the murderer's own hands. Whose psychic excitement in the commission of the crime is increased a hundredfold!'

'Why are you staring at me — ?' Darrell demanded, his fingers clenching convulsively.

'Those latent fingerprints are chemically more permanent that they might be ordinarily,' Doctor Morelle continued relentlessly, his cold gaze unwavering. 'Permanent enough to withstand water, however hot. Up to five hundred degrees Centigrade.'

Miss Frayle had moved to the telephone. 'I suppose I dial O and get the Exchange — ' she began, and picked up the instrument.

'Put down that phone!' Darrell cried, and took a menacing step towards Miss Frayle.

'What do you — ?' Startled, Miss Frayle let the instrument clatter back onto its rest, but retained her grip on it.

She glanced wildly at Doctor Morelle, who had risen to his feet, but was stood watching impassively.

Darrell moved another step forward, his hands slightly extended before him, fingers twitching in a threatening manner.

'Put it down, or I'll wipe you out, too!'

'What — ?' Miss Frayle stammered, taking a step back, and raising her arm protectively before her.

Darrell took another step. 'I wasn't going to let that old fool cut me out again — ' He halted, as Miss Frayle's frightened expression inexplicably changed to one of relief.

'Oh, Mr. Redford — !'

Darrell spun round, to see that Redford had entered the room, and, after taking in the situation, was rushing purposefully towards him.

'So it was *you* — !'

'What the — *Aaargh*!' Darrell's snarl of anger ended in a grunt of intense pain, as the rose bowl suddenly descended on the back of his head with a tremendous thump.

He crumpled, sprawling to the floor,

where he lay in a small pool of water, his head and shoulders garlanded with the scattered blooms as Doctor Morelle let go of the rose bowl he had dextrously wielded.

'Oh, Doctor Morelle!' Miss Frayle gasped, in mingled relief and admiration. 'You saved me.'

Smiling thinly, Doctor Morelle glanced down at the still figure. 'That should serve to keep him quiet until the police arrive.'

Following his gaze, Redford nodded. 'He's out cold.' Then he glanced up at the Doctor. 'But how did you know? What put you on to him?'

Doctor Morelle smiled sardonically. 'Miss Frayle can explain — '

'It came to me in a flash,' Miss Frayle said, smiling brightly.

'Very brave of you not to move from the phone,' Radford remarked.

Miss Frayle puffed with pride. 'Doctor Morelle asked me to get the police and I always obey his instructions.'

'But you haven't obeyed, Miss Frayle,' the Doctor murmured dryly.

'Eh?' Miss Frayle gave a little start. 'Oh, no — in the excitement I quite forgot. The way you caught him with that bowl of roses, Doctor Morelle!'

'Pretty quick of you,' Redford remarked.

Doctor Morelle permitted himself a slight smile of satisfaction. 'I was grateful to you for distracting his attention, coming in as you did at a critical moment.'

'I came back to ask you which you'd prefer, tea or coffee.'

'Oh, tea please.' Miss Frayle looked at Redford, then added chattily: 'Doctor Morelle and I always have tea when we work late at night.'

'Are you getting the police, Miss Frayle?' Doctor Morelle asked, with a touch of impatience.

'Let me do it, Miss Frayle.' Redford moved towards where she stood — somewhat unsteadily — by the phone.

'Oh, thank you. I do feel a bit sort of overexcited.' She moved to a nearby chair and sank into it gratefully.

Redford dialled, then: 'Exchange? Put me on to Wimbledon Police Station . . . '

Doctor Morelle returned to his seat and regarded Miss Frayle paternally.

'Yes, Doctor,' she said, 'I suddenly realised that he must have left his fingerprints when he gripped the poor old man's ankles.'

Doctor Morelle smiled faintly and glanced at the unmoving manservant. 'He was certainly under that impression too.'

Miss Frayle detected the note of sarcasm. 'What do you mean? You agreed with me. You said how even hot water wouldn't remove them. Up to five hundred degrees Centigrade — '

'I took advantage of the fear your observation obviously aroused in him,' Doctor Morelle said suavely.

'But — ?' Miss Frayle's bafflement was evident.

'Fingerprints can remain, after immersion in hot water,' Doctor Morelle explained patiently. '*But they do not even appear on the surface of human skin!*'

'But if it wasn't the hint I gave you, what was it — ?'

Before Doctor Morelle could answer

Miss Frayle's question Redford cut in: 'The police are on their way, and should be here very soon.'

'Good,' Doctor Morelle murmured.

Redford glanced down at the still figure of Darrell. 'What made you realise it was him?'

'Your uncle had asked Darrell to witness the changed will tomorrow. He knew at once that he was being cut out of the present will, which left him five thousand pounds. No one can witness a will from which they may benefit.'

'Why, of course — ' Redford smiled.

'Then my idea about the fingerprints was all wrong?' Miss Frayle asked ruefully.

Doctor Morelle gave her an almost kindly look. 'I fear so, Miss Frayle.' He turned to Redford, and added: 'Your aunt, by the same reasoning, Mr. Redford, your aunt was obviously not implicated. For all she knew she might benefit from the new will.'

'Yes, I see that now.'

'But the roses,' Miss Frayle said slowly, thinking. 'That bowl of roses. Don't they have some connection with what's happened?'

'Only that Mr. Redford doesn't appear to have notice their presence,' Doctor Morelle smiled.

'Why that's true!' Redford exclaimed. 'I haven't.'

'Which merely proved to me that your fear that you might be responsible for your uncle's death was no longer present in your subconscious,' Doctor Morelle pronounced. 'Therefore I knew that you, at least, Mr. Redford, had no guilty secret in connection with tonight's murder.'

6

The case of the Perfect Wife

Deep in the recesses of Miss Frayle's subconscious there lingers persistently positive regrets that the Doctor had ever undertaken one certain case. The mystery had not been, in itself, any more consciously terrifying, bizarre, or replete with more violence and danger than many other adventures upon which she had accompanied Doctor Morelle. On the surface she has seemingly long since forgotten the affair, on the principle that the human memory, like the sundial, registers only the sunny hours. If one asked her why she never wishes to refer to it again, she would quite honestly be unable to answer.

However, perhaps the impartial observer, who is also an intelligent analyst of the fascinating bypaths of human behaviourism will be able himself to solve the mystery of the deep frustration in Miss Frayle's other mind, following the strange events referred to. The relevant facts and details are itemised in the subsequent chronicle, and although the factual mystery is elucidated the psychological one is left to be solved by the observer.

Associations indelibly connected with the case in Miss Frayle's subconscious were manifested in the early Spring when the trees in Regent's Park, a few minutes' walk from Doctor Morelle's house in Harley Street, were breaking into leaf, and the boats and red-sailed yachts on the lake were being repainted for the fine weather to come. London, after dreary months of fog, snow and rain took on a new and stimulating charm. People were ready to smile. They shed their worries as they shed their topcoats.

Miss Frayle with her unsubtle emotions and sympathies, greeted spring in the obvious and wisest way, with a lightness of heart and a recklessness towards bright colours in her mode of dress. Even Doctor Morelle, though more impassive and phlegmatic in his enthusiasms, also registered the arrival of the seasonal rebirth. One day when she came into the study silently, he was actually humming to himself — though he quickly ceased when he observed her. For the past week, too, he had displayed restrained, yet unmistakable good humour. Recriminations, sardonic chuckles, thin smiles and biting sarcasm had been noticeably rare in his manner.

The orientation of the Doctor's good humour signified itself in a single action that came as a pleasant and unexpected shock to Miss Frayle. She discovered that he had added to her weekly pay-cheque a bonus of no less than five pounds!

Delightedly she cashed this cheque, and because the sun was shining at that moment, recklessly drew out some additional money from her Post Office Savings. Thus armed, on her first free afternoon she gaily tripped along New Bond Street. She entered a beauty establishment, where she suffered herself to undergo the masochistic delights of a mudpack and a permanent wave. Before she left she received expert advice from a charming matron on how to make the best of herself — how cosmetics discreetly applied could enhance her natural charm. She was not satisfied until she entered another shop and bought an attractive two-piece of light grey material with pin stripe. Miss Frayle's transformation was not yet quite complete. In an oculist's window she observed pink shell spectacle frames. Before the small voice of conscience had time to whisper about extravagance, she walked in and asked the man behind the counter if it was possible for him to remove her present lenses from their dark frames, and insert them in the pink shell ones. Nothing, apparently, could be more simple.

It was not until she was approaching the Doctor's study that she was seized with apprehension. Suppose he made some caustic comment about her transformation? It might well break his unexpected sequence of good humour if he accused her of spending the bonus foolishly. He might say something sarcastic and so painfully true, in his hypercritical way, that she would be impelled never to wear the pink-rimmed spectacles again, she might be impelled to flatten the expensive waves in her hair. Or perhaps he would not notice any change in her at all! She sighed.

However, she pulled herself together, and with head high, entered the study. He was bent intently over some notes at his desk. He did not raise his head. She fussed around the study, tidying things unnecessarily and occasionally asking questions. He answered only in monosyllables, without looking at her.

At last — it seemed an eternity to her — he had occasion to glance in her direction. The glance became a stare, and his eyes narrowed as they bent upon her.

'Do I detect a metamorphosis in your appearance, Miss Frayle?'

She simulated a casual little laugh.

'Oh, you mean this suit and my new hair style,' she cooed, and added gaily, 'Like it?'

His stare travelled analytically from her hair to her well-shod feet; she found the suspense unbearable.

He turned to his notes again.

'It is not unbecoming,' he said.

She breathed in relief. A blush of pleasure suffused her smooth cheeks. This was praise indeed from the impassive and censorious Doctor. However, the final hallmark of approval was to be evinced a little later, when, after lunch, she returned to her desk, to find a small bunch of exquisite lilies-of-the-valley beside her typewriter. Could this charming present possibly be a gift from the Doctor? It seemed incredible.

When he returned she asked him:

'Have I you to thank for these charming flowers, Doctor?'

He peered laconically through the window and spoke over his shoulder.

'I felt that they might add to the aesthetic value of your ensemble,' he said casually, 'perhaps they might alleviate any slight suggestion of — er — severity.'

Murmuring her thanks, she pinned the delicate flowers high on her left shoulder and faced him with a radiant smile.

'Is this how I should wear them?' she asked.

He nodded, but made no reply. Next

moment he had launched into a spasm of dictation, hardly giving her time to procure her notebook and pencil.

The following day found the Doctor and Miss Frayle driving through the picturesque roads and lanes of Surrey on their way to attend an urgent call from an old patient. The visit was purely a routine one and of no special interest. In the late afternoon they were returning to town by car again. Miss Frayle, radiant in her new finery, was sitting in the front next to the Doctor.

She peered over her shoulder and then turned sharply to him.

'There's a car coming behind us at a terrific speed,' she warned. 'It's swerving all over the road and — ' Her words were drowned by the insistent blare from a Klaxon horn. 'Listen to the beastly thing!'

He drew well over to the left side.

'The driver seems to suffer from the delusion the highway was built exclusively for him — or her,' he observed.

'I think I should pull over to the side,' she advised anxiously.

'Indeed. Miss Frayle, I have already

done so,' he murmured.

'Here it comes!' she exclaimed, and held her breath.

The car — a dusty-cream high-powered roadster, tore past them at a terrific speed, with the horn blaring maddeningly. Already it was disappearing into the distance.

'What a way to drive!' exclaimed Miss Frayle indignantly. 'Absolutely mad!' She smiled brightly towards the Doctor. 'Anyway, you'll be glad to know it was a woman! I saw her as she went by.'

'A woman!' he repeated with marked scorn. 'I had apprehended as much, only a female or a person mentally deranged could proceed in such a manner.'

'It's just as well it's a lonely road,' she commented, 'or she'd be bound to hit something.'

He slackened the pace of his car. Then carefully he ran it on to the grass verge, and applied the brakes.

'As we have already paused in our journey, Miss Frayle, and the hour indicates luncheon time,' he noted, not unpleasantly, 'I feel we may well choose this moment to produce the sandwiches and thermos flask before proceeding further.'

'Good idea, Doctor,' she agreed enthusiastically. 'I'm really quite hungry . . . ' She reached down for the picnic basket, and lifted out a package covered with a table napkin. 'Here you are, here are the sandwiches.'

'I hope they are thinly cut, as I requested?'

'Yes. And now for the thermos flask!'

After the picnic lunch they proceeded on their journey.

'I must confess, Miss Frayle,' he observed, 'I found that little repast most refreshing.'

'I'm so glad, Doctor.'

He gazed ahead at sunlight through the trees.

'The resumption of the journey is quite pleasurable,' he observed.

'One feels better after a good meal, I always think,' she said unoriginally.

'The sandwiches were indeed both appetising and nutritious,' he vouchsafed.

'I thought they were nice too,' she remarked chattily, 'though I suppose I shouldn't say so — '

'Indeed? And why not?' He raised his eyebrows quizzically as he gave her a sidelong glance. 'Or am I to infer from your remarks and that air of modest self-effacement that you were responsible for the refreshment?'

'Yes, I *did* make them myself,' she announced proudly.

'Hm. Well, they were still very acceptable.' And they lapsed into silence.

Miss Frayle sank lower into her seat, the gentle warmth of the afternoon, and the soft purr of the car engine, lulling her to a state of drowsiness. She sat up abruptly, however, when, a few minutes later, she heard the Doctor exclaim:

'Ah! What is this I perceive ahead?'

'What is it? What's the matter?'

'Kindly apply your powers of observation to the hedgerow at this fork in the road we are approaching.'

She looked ahead to a gap in the hedgerow near a sharp turn.

'Gracious! It looks as though something's driven right through it!' she commented in alarm.

'Precisely, Miss Frayle. I feel an investigation is indicated.'

He applied his brakes and pulled up a few yards from the gap. Miss Frayle got out of the car first and stared fixedly at the road surface.

'Look!' she exclaimed. 'These skid marks in the road.'

'I am just coming to note the details,' he replied, as he alighted from the car. 'Hm . . . Yes, I think we shall find it was a motor vehicle that drove through the hedge. It must have been travelling at high speed.'

Miss Frayle suddenly clutched her throat in anxiety. Her eyes widened tensely. 'That woman in the car? Do you think it's her — ? Oh dear!'

He nodded impassively. 'It had occurred to me the female at the wheel of that juggernaut is the responsible party.'

'We'd better look,' she said urgently. 'The poor woman may have injured herself!'

He was already proceeding across a grass verge. Adroitly he stepped over the flattened hedge.

'Let us proceed through the aperture made by the machine,' he directed. 'Ah, there is a slope on the other side. Take precautions that you do not slip.'

She was gingerly following him.

'Tyre tracks of the car. Look!' she pointed. 'It must have rushed on down.'

'Fortunately it is not a precipitous incline, merely a slight dip.'

Miss Frayle placed a hand mariner-fashion over her eyes to shield them from the sun-glare, and she looked ahead across a field. She saw the car, pulled up, still upright on its four wheels, but tilted slightly at an angle.

'There it is, over there. Look, Doctor,' she cried.

'I am suffering from neither deficiency in hearing nor vision, Miss Frayle!' he retorted surprisingly with only a hint of exasperation. 'I had observed the car in question halted some hundred yards away halfway up the opposite incline.'

'Let's hurry there, in case anything's happened!' Already she was stumbling quickly across the field. He followed at a slower pace.

'I think it unlikely the driver or vehicle can have suffered much harm, though possibly we may render some assistance in directing the machine back to the road.'

'Do let's be quick, though, just in case — ' she panted.

A few seconds later, distinctly breathless, he began to protest. 'Really, Miss Frayle, such haste is not at all necessary in the circumstances.'

'I can see the woman in the car, Doctor! She's very still — !'

'Doubtless stunned slightly or overcome with shock.'

'I do hope — ' she flung her hands out to him for support. He steadied her absently. 'Oh, dear, I nearly tripped up! I do hope she's all right.'

'The answer will be vouchsafed in a moment.'

She hoisted herself on to the running board.

'Oh look — ! She's — she's — '

The woman lay slumped over in the driving seat. A heavy black mark showed on her forehead, Miss Frayle drew back as she realised the truth. Meanwhile the Doctor climbed into the car and conducted his examination.

'Hm. I'm afraid — '

'She's — she's dead, Doctor?'

He nodded grimly. 'She has suffered a tremendous blow on the head. As you see here — '

She could not bring herself to look at the dead woman. She gazed wildly around her as though seeking further help.

'But how can it have happened — ?' She broke off; and pointed agitatedly across the field. 'The branch of that tree down there in the dip! It's hanging very low, and it's right in the path of the car as it rushed along. It's an open car and — '

'You are becoming acutely observant!'

'That's how it *must* have happened, isn't it?' she asked anxiously.

He nodded, as he applied his lighter to the tip of a Le Sphinx. 'I might be inclined to agree with your hypothesis.' He leaned over the side of the car again. 'There is, however, another important factor. Have you also observed that a slight trickle of oil is dripping from the steering column?'

This time she forced herself to look at the recumbent body in the ear.

'Yes — yes, I can see that, Doctor,' she said in a hushed, awe-stricken tone.

'You might examine the position of the oil spots more closely, Miss Frayle. What do they signify to you?'

'The — the spots are on the left edge of the coat near the knee, that's all.'

'Nothing more?' he queried. 'Glance back for a moment towards that tree in the dip with the overhanging branch. Some fifty yards distant — '

'Doctor Morelle, what has it all to do with this poor woman? The exact positions of the oil-stains on her coat, and — ' she gave a sudden gasp of realisation. 'Oh! You — you don't mean — she hasn't been — it isn't — ?'

'Precisely that, my dear Miss Frayle. A case of homicide. Very cunning. Diabolically cunning, but not quite cunning enough.'

'But how can you know it's — it's murder? She was alone in the car, and — '

He clicked his tongue impatiently.

'From the clues which have presented themselves, and from the factors to which I have taken pains to draw your attention, the truth should be evident — '

'I still can't see, Doctor, but then I never can. Please explain.'

'There is no time for explanations now,' he snapped. 'The perpetrator cannot be far away from this vicinity. We must apprehend him.'

'You mean we're going — going on a murder hunt?'

'Precisely.'

'But suppose the man's desperate? He might be armed and — ' she speculated wildly.

'That is a contingency we must face.' He stamped out the stub of his cigarette. 'But first of all, it behoves us to ascertain the identity of the deceased.'

'There is a library book in that little recess, just there by the dashboard,' she indicated. 'That might help.'

He lifted the book. A token was attached by a piece of twine to a loop of wire at the top of the volume. His eyes narrowed as he scanned some words typewritten on the card.

'Mrs. Roger Horniblow,' he read. 'Hm . . . A Chelsea address.'

'Horniblow!' echoed Miss Frayle. She pressed her forehead with a clenched hand in an effort of concentration. 'Where have I heard the name — I've seen it — or read about it somewhere.'

'Would she be a theatrical personage? Or perhaps a cinema actress — ?'

'No — no, I'd know the name immediately if she was,' she pondered. 'Let me think — I know! She's — she's — ' she broke off.

'Yes? Exactly who and what is she?'

'She's the Perfect Wife, Doctor!' Miss Frayle exclaimed. 'There was all that publicity and — oh, you must have read it. But no, of course, you wouldn't. It was in the popular press — the *Daily Tribune*, that's it. There were columns about her and her husband every day for weeks — '

'And with what cretinous purpose?' he demanded smoothly.

'The *Daily Tribune* offered a prize of

£10 a week for life for the Perfect Marriage. They invited people to send in claims. Retired High Court Judges were commissioned to judge the claims — '

'What a monstrous travesty of judicial dignity!' the Doctor commented acidly.

'Anyway, Mrs. Horniblow's marriage was judged to be the Perfect Marriage,' she continued, 'and she was voted the Perfect Wife, and he was the Perfect Husband. It was — well, it was all perfect. The *Tribune* gave day-to-day accounts of the Horniblows' married life — with pictures and everything. I remember how much I envied — ' She broke off and said in a dismayed whisper, 'And there — there she lies, the Perfect Wife, murdered!'

'Evidently the fierce light of publicity beating upon her marriage throne was too revealing — judging from the subsequent happenings,' he observed cynically. 'However, we have established her identity. Now we must discover the whereabouts of the murderer.'

Miss Frayle imagined she saw moving shadows in a clump of trees.

'Do you think he might be hiding over there — in that wood, watching us?' she speculated, then gave a timorous squeak. 'Perhaps with a rifle trained on us at this moment!'

Doctor Morelle laughed shortly. 'He is far more likely to be seeking some form of locomotion which would take him as far as possible away from the scene of the crime.' He started to walk, with long, raking strides, towards the gap in the hedge, calling over his shoulder, 'Come, Miss Frayle, let us proceed to London by the normal route.'

'And leave poor Mrs. Horniblow here?'

'Regrettably we can do nothing for her.'

They returned to the Doctor's car. As they drove off, he was scanning the road ahead. He peered eagerly when he saw a male figure standing hesitantly by some crossroads.

'Now, Miss Frayle, you would no doubt recognise Mrs. Horniblow's husband from his photographs in the journals, would you not?'

'I think so.'

'Then kindly inform me, when we draw

closer to this man, whether he is indeed Mr. Horniblow.'

'I'd better signal to you,' she agreed intriguingly. 'I know, I'll give a little cough.'

The man, on seeing the car approaching, threw a suspicious look at them, and at that moment Miss Frayle saw him full-featured — a handsome, clean-cut man of about thirty.

She coughed. The Doctor took no notice. She coughed again ostentatiously.

'Quiet, Miss Frayle!' he snapped.

He drew the car to a standstill.

'Can I offer you a lift?'

'Why, yes — if you're going to London,' the man nodded, and climbed in the back. 'Jolly decent of you.'

Miss Frayle tried to stifle an inclination to shudder, as she realised that the man sitting behind her was no doubt a murderer. He looked disarming enough in appearance, but she remembered how, often enough, it had been dinned into her by the Doctor that appearances were often deceptive.

'I've been cooling my heels at that

corner for the last half hour,' the man volunteered. 'Been waiting for my wife to pick me up in the car. I dare say she's lost herself. You know how irresponsible women are when they have their hands on the steering wheel.'

'We did see a female driving a cream-coloured open car,' observed the Doctor. 'She passed us several miles down the road.'

'That would be my wife,' the man replied. He scratched his head with every appearance of puzzlement. 'Odd, that she didn't come past the crossroads. Ah well, she must have taken another turning. I dare say she'll be home when I get there.'

Miss Frayle thought: 'He's trying to establish an alibi for himself.' By his very frankness he was disarming suspicion. No doubt when he learnt of his wife's death, he would simulate intense grief. Miss Frayle accepted completely the Doctor's statement that Mrs. Horniblow had been murdered in some ingenious manner. But, although she re-pieced the clues, she could not discover how he had elucidated this. For the solution to the mystery she would have to wait until he had an opportunity to enlighten her.

Through the windscreen mirror she watched their passenger light a cigarette. His hand shook, though he made a passable display of nonchalance as he drew and exhaled.

'My name's Horniblow,' the man volunteered cheerily. 'You may have heard the name. The missus and I had our pictures in the paper — quite a lot of fuss — '

'The Perfect Married Couple,' Miss Frayle ventured. 'Yes, I remember.'

The Doctor permitted himself a sardonic chuckle.

'And what would you describe as the most important factor in compatible marital relationships, Mr. Horniblow?' he queried.

'Give and take — and a sense of humour.' Horniblow gave a laugh that had a subtly bitter timbre. 'And a few quarrels!' he went on enigmatically. 'The missus and I just quarrel over trifles and agree about the big things. It's fun making up after a little quarrel.'

'I can quite imagine it,' declared Miss Frayle.

'I'd like you both to come to dinner with us some time,' went on the other, emboldened by their show of interest. 'We've a little maisonette just off Sloane Street.'

'That is indeed fortuitous,' the Doctor murmured and added prevaricatingly, 'I garage my vehicle in that vicinity, so I will be able to convey you directly to your home.'

'That's jolly decent of you. I'm rather anxious to get there — a bit worried what's happened to the missus, you know.'

The Doctor encouraged the man to chatter about his happily married life as the car was moving into the thick of the traffic on the fringe of London. A sudden mist reduced visibility, and darkness had now fallen. A few minutes later the Doctor was driving down Whitehall. He was congratulating himself that the passenger had evidently not noticed he was taking a rather circuitous route to Sloane Street.

He swung the car through an archway

and applied the brakes.

'Perhaps, before we proceed, you will join me in a little — er stimulant,' he asked cordially.

'Why, I'd be glad to — '

Horniblow peered into the half-light. 'Do you live here?'

'Not exactly. It is merely a rendezvous which I find extremely congenial.'

Miss Frayle's heart raced as the Doctor led them through one of the side doors at Scotland Yard, and through a door marked 'Private'. Sitting at his desk was the genial Detective-Inspector Hood. Horniblow drew back mystified. But the Doctor's manner was so disarming that for Horniblow to have hurriedly left would have aroused suspicion.

'Is this a social call, Doctor?' asked Inspector Hood with a wide smile.

'Assuredly. I want you to meet an acquaintance of mine.'

'I say — I thought we were going into a club or a pub — not Scotland Yard,' Horniblow exclaimed with a mixture of blank amazement and indignation.

'Well, if it's a drink you want, I might

fix it,' the Inspector smiled. 'Any friend of the Doctor's is a friend of mine.'

He extended a large hand, and while he was shaking Horniblow's hand cordially, the Doctor remarked casually.

'Mr. Horniblow has a statement to make, relative to his wife who has been the victim of homicide!'

'What — ! Why you — ?'

The Inspector's grip changed to an iron grip as the other tried to break away with a stream of oaths and curses. Doctor Morelle merely lit a Le Sphinx and chuckled sardonically. He could not judge who was the more surprised, Horniblow or the Inspector.

'Perhaps you will detain him for questioning, while I enunciate the details.' He turned to Miss Frayle with a thin smile. 'Will you kindly wait in the car?'

* * *

An hour later in his Harley Street study, Doctor Morelle was awaiting a telephone call from Scotland Yard. At last the bell rang, and Detective-Inspector

Hood was on the line.

'You were right, Doctor, Horniblow did murder his wife. He's just confessed. Apparently their marriage wasn't so perfect after all. There was another woman in the case, and Horniblow couldn't desert his wife without having to give up the ten pounds a week pension from the newspaper.'

When Doctor Morelle replaced the receiver, he moved across to his favourite high-backed armchair, and sat down with the obvious satisfaction of a good day's work smoothly executed.

Miss Frayle walked round from her desk and stood against the mantelpiece, under the light, where she knew that her new clothes and aids to beauty would be revealed to the best advantage.

'I'm still wondering how you knew it was murder,' she prompted dutifully.

He extinguished a half-smoked Le Sphinx.

'The vital clue which pointed to the woman in the car having been murdered was the fact that the car had stopped halfway up the incline,' he declared. 'If

230

the overhanging branch in the dip had struck the woman's head and killed her it's quite likely the vehicle would have continued up the opposite incline, but it would inevitably have rolled down again since the woman would naturally have been unable to apply the brakes.'

'And all that talk about the oil stains on the poor woman's coat was just, well, talk — eh, Doctor?'

'Not exactly, Miss Frayle. We had apparently seen the deceased driving the car earlier on, but the position of the oil stains gave me reason to doubt it was her at all. They were on the left edge of the garment, whereas a woman wraps her coat over from right to left, and the right edge would have been exposed to the oil drips.'

'You mean it was the husband we saw masquerading as the woman — who was hidden in the car already dead?'

'Precisely,' he nodded. 'It was all ingeniously devised to lend colour to the accident scheme.'

'How perfectly horrid,' she exclaimed. She paused, and then said: 'But fancy your noticing which way a woman wraps her coat, Doctor.'

He smiled faintly. 'Indeed I may never have done so if *you* had not bought such striking and becoming new apparel!'

'Oh, thank you!'

'On this occasion you were unintentionally most useful,' he said, surprisingly, and added at a tangent: 'Incidentally, Miss Frayle, I feel you are somewhat in need of a change of scene and environment. I imagine, too, a rest after my labours would benefit *me*.'

She gazed at him, her lips parted.

'Doctor Morelle, are we going off on a holiday?' she speculated delightedly. 'What a lovely idea!'

He coughed, and looked away from her. Miss Frayle suddenly thought he was displaying embarrassment for the first time in his life.

'I hope — er — '

'Yes, Doctor?'

'I hoped you would appreciate the suggestion. I was — er — wondering if the scenery of the Lake District would appeal to you — ?'

Her eyes sparkled radiantly.

'Simply wonderful,' she enthused. 'I should love it!'

'I am gratified it meets with your approval,' he observed. 'I have already bought the tickets.'

She looked up at him with starry eyes.

'Lovely lakes and mountains! Oh, we shall have a glorious time there together!'

'I have also made you out a small cheque as a contribution towards any extraneous expenses you may have to incur in connection with your vacation,' he continued

'No, Doctor. You're much too kind,' she protested. 'I don't think I can accept — '

'Not at all!' he retorted. 'It gives me great pleasure. Here is your cheque and railway ticket.' He rose from his chair and stood by the window, gazing out at the street lamps in Harley Street, and added over his shoulder: 'Unfortunately mountains affect me with dizziness, so I shall not, my dear Miss Frayle, be accompanying you. I am taking my holidays elsewhere.'

Miss Frayle's jaw dropped. She touched

the lilies-of-the-valley on her shoulder. Then she grasped them impulsively and snatched them from their pin.

Ever since she has been curiously allergic to lilies-of-the-valley . . . though *why* she cannot consciously explain to herself, or anyone else. But there are moments when a glimpse of her subconscious is revealed to her. It is then she seems to connect the Case of the Perfect Wife with her dislike for lilies-of-the-valley.

THE END

We do hope that you have enjoyed reading this large print book.

Did you know that all of our titles are available for purchase?

We publish a wide range of high quality large print books including:
Romances, Mysteries, Classics
General Fiction
Non Fiction and Westerns

Special interest titles available in large print are:
The Little Oxford Dictionary
Music Book, Song Book
Hymn Book, Service Book

Also available from us courtesy of Oxford University Press:
Young Readers' Dictionary
(large print edition)
Young Readers' Thesaurus
(large print edition)

For further information or a free brochure, please contact us at:
Ulverscroft Large Print Books Ltd.,
The Green, Bradgate Road, Anstey,
Leicester, LE7 7FU, England.
Tel: (00 44) **0116 236 4325**
Fax: (00 44) **0116 234 0205**

Other titles in the
Linford Mystery Library:

F.B.I. SPECIAL AGENT

Gordon Landsborough

Cheyenne Charlie, Native American law student turned G-Man, is one of the Bureau's top agents. The New York office sends for him to investigate a sinister criminal gang called the Blond Boys. Their getaway cars somehow disappear in well-lit streets; they jam police radios; and now they've begun to add brutal murder to their daring robberies. Cheyenne follows a tangled trail that leads him to a desperate fight to the death in the beautiful scenery of the Catskill Mountains . . .

RED CENTRE

Frederick Nolan

Moscow, 1986. The Chief Intelligence Directorate of the Soviet General Staff is preparing to launch the Death Bird, an ultra-secret assault satellite. A pre-emptive measure to ensure the West could never place in orbit any satellite deemed inimical to Soviet interests . . . And in the technological world of espionage, treachery, betrayal and sudden death, only British secret agent David Caine and the lovely Cuban-America widow Lynda Sanchez can prevent the master spy from achieving his ends . . .

THE WALL

E. C. Tubb

Business associates Kerron, Chang and Forrest, three of the richest men on Earth, are old and approaching the end of their days. Desperate to prolong their lives, they seek the man who seems to have the secret of immortality: the mysterious Brett, an adventurer who has apparently lived for centuries. But Brett hides a dark secret . . . and for him to help them, they must accompany him on the most dangerous journey — to the centre of the Galaxy — beyond the Wall!

DEATH SMELLS OF CORDITE

Gordon Landsborough

Big Russ Farran is a millionaire who owns the Farran industrial empire. But he isn't so big when he finds an ex-G-man lying with a neat hole in his head. Now he's wanted by the cops and the FBI and, accused of murder, Farran's millions are no help to him. He must save himself. But first he must solve the mystery of who his enemy is — that ruthless, scheming mastermind who's framed him, and who wants his millions . . .

SHADOW OF THE WOLF

Michael Parker

1943. The Allies and Hitler's Nazi Germany fight the battle of the Atlantic. German commandos land on North Cape Island, off the north coast of Scotland. And Bruno Schafer's orders are to find a missing U boat captain with information regarding Britain's new centimetric radar. The islanders, remnants of a once thriving whaling community, deny the man's existence. However, only youngsters Billy and Ailie and an old whale catching boat, the Nordcaper, stand against Schafer succeeding in his mission.